TELL ME ALL YOUR LIES

IN THE CAROLINAS
BOOK 4

ANGEL ANDERS

Published by Angel Anders
Editing by Steph White (Kat's Literary Services)
Proofreading by Vanessa Esquibel (Kat's Literary Services)
Cover designed by Maldo Designs

To fighting for the life you want and getting it on your own terms. Here's to happily ever afters that break the mold.

ONE

Cara

"I'M GOING TO KILL HIM." I huff as I slouch in my black leather office chair.

"No, you won't," Ruby says with a light laugh.

Ruby gets out of her seat from across my desk and heads over to my espresso maker. She starts making me a latte, which usually helps calm my nerves instead of spiking them.

As my longtime assistant, she's attuned to my wants and needs at all times, even when I haven't gotten there yet.

Ruby stays focused on the coffee machine as it starts to dispense the espresso shot, followed by the steaming milk.

"I think I will, actually," I say matter-of-factly as I sit upright.

Slouching is for the weak, and I am not weak. Frustrated or stressed may be words to describe how I feel, but I won't say them out loud with Ruby here. She'll just smile knowingly.

"You can't."

"Why? He's just another man in my way."

Ruby shakes her auburn hair as she stirs my latte.

"You know why."

She gives me that knowing look as she approaches the desk, sets the coffee mug down, and retakes her seat across from me.

Ruby looks down at her tablet and begins scrolling through my daily agenda. Right to business, even while I'm still stewing from what happened.

"You have the call with Mr. Ross coming up in ten minutes. I emailed you the final documentation. Have you had a chance to look it over yet?" Ruby peers up from the tablet.

"I *can* kill him."

She sighs and shrugs her shoulders before focusing back on the tablet.

"What's with the shrugging?" I ask.

I lean forward and tent my fingers against my mouth as my elbows rest on my desk, waiting for her to tell me why she's disagreeing with me this much. Usually, Ruby speaks her mind, but when it comes to this one man in particular, she doesn't hold back.

Taking off her bright purple glasses, she rubs the sides of her nose at the indentation marks.

"Am I bothering you?" I ask.

She glares at me for the interruption and then starts to wipe her glasses with the hem of her sweater.

"You *can't* kill him for two important reasons."

She puts her glasses back on as I sit more upright, ready to hear her reasoning about this matter.

"Oh, please. Do share what the two reasons are as to

why I can't kill my archnemesis, who always seems to be in my way."

She gives me a pointed look as she grips the edge of her tablet.

"For one, he's one of your dad's closest friends. I would dare say his best friend."

"Fine. Only you're forgetting that my dad doesn't know what it is both of us do."

That brings a smirk from across the desk.

"Since that isn't actually a deal-breaker as to why I can't kill him... what's your second reason?"

Another sharp look.

"What? You did specify you have two reasons."

Ruby grins as she looks back down at the tablet and begins tapping. After a moment, she looks back up at me.

"It's obvious, isn't it?"

"Apparently not to me."

That smug grin is back in place.

"It's simple. You're going to marry that man one day."

My mouth pops open as I look at my assistant like she has a dozen heads. Regrouping, it's my turn to give her a cutting stare.

"I'm *not* getting married."

Ruby shakes her head slightly and then focuses back on the tablet.

"I'm *not*. Marriage is not for me."

She doesn't look up from the device as I continue to stew.

"That's fine. You're right, and I'm wrong."

"It's not about me being right. I'm simply never getting married."

"Okay, so you're never getting married because who needs love and a partner?" she responds rhetorically.

"Love isn't in the cards for me, but you know what is?"

Ruby finally looks up at me.

"What's that?"

"Catching the Kingpin of Charlotte. Once I get the person, then I'll get their boss too. And I'm not going to let *Grant Sinclair* get in the way of that."

"I will say this," Ruby says.

I nod to encourage her to continue.

"Two things can be true at the same time."

I slink back in my chair and close my eyes as I pinch the bridge of my nose.

"Let's go over the rest of your list after my call with Mr. Ross. I'm surprised the agency is calling me again so soon."

"No, you aren't," Ruby answers with a laugh.

I sit back upright in my chair, and a wide smile fills my face.

"You're right; I'm not."

The agency needs me just as much as its director seems to.

Ruby gets out of her chair and pushes it inward.

"I'll pop back in after your call. I do need to know what you want to wear to your parents' gala tomorrow night. I only have a small window to go shopping for you today."

I groan as she starts to head to my door.

"You have to go," she laments.

"But *he* will be there."

"Yes, and maybe you'll have something to gloat about?"

"It never works that way with Grant."

She looks over her shoulder and smiles.

"I am *not* going to marry him one day," I repeat.

"See you shortly," she singsongs as she leaves my office.

With the shut of the door, I'm left alone once more. I'm used to the quiet as much as I'm used to the hustle that comes with being a private security contractor. My days and nights are usually busy, giving me ample time to get lost in work.

It's not every day that a woman is able to climb the ladder in this field, and I'm proud that I busted my ass to get here. The government comes to me for help; I've put away countless criminals, and I've done it all in heels.

Glancing at my computer clock, I only have a few minutes to prep for the call with Dodger Ross, the agency's director.

Dodger and I have a precarious relationship—one where we both need each other despite our best interests. It all stems from a complicated past that started over fifteen years ago.

We met my freshman year at California University and immediately hit it off. It was a coincidence that we were in all the same classes that year, but then, each year that followed, we did our best to stay together as we progressed.

One of the reasons we connected so easily was because of our respective drives to be successful. Dodger could have easily been the person I'm calling my archnemesis today if it wasn't for the way we bonded that first year studying for exams in the library.

After much hard work, we were finally about to graduate college when it happened. Dodger and I both had heard that CU was one of the top colleges to attend if you wanted to be recruited by the agency. When I found out I had been accepted to CU, I cried tears of joy. It's one of the only times I remember crying as an adult.

Anyone who wanted to get into the agency had to graduate top of their class at one of three major universities designed to test potential recruits.

One night while studying during our freshman year, we

admitted that was both of our goals for post-graduation. Becoming an agent with the agency was everything I wanted, proving that not only was I smart but I had what it took to accomplish such a feat.

As soon as I walked off the graduation stage, I knew I was going to be recruited. Two agents stood in the wings waiting, and it was obvious what they were doing there.

Since my last name began with a C, I was asked first. Dodger would later tell me he didn't know where I had gone when he didn't see me back in my seat as he walked up to the stage.

The same situation happened to him. As soon as he walked off, two different agents were there to recruit him for their program. The rest is history, as they say. Well, I wish I could say that's true. Dodger's and my relationship began to unravel after that.

When we both discovered we were in their recruitment program, it was one of the best days of our lives. Everything we dreamed of was happening: being able to remain best friends while becoming agents.

We had successfully gone through the program, and it was the last night before we would be getting our assignments when it all fell apart. Dodger admitted to me that night that he had romantic feelings for me. I should have seen it coming, but I truly didn't. If I had, I would have set more boundaries between us to try and preserve the friendship.

All through college and training, I thought we were just friends, but clearly Dodger didn't. He waited until he knew we would be going our separate ways to make a move. Looking back, I assume it was in case I turned him down after he admitted the truth.

It was a tough position to be in, but I respected him so

much that I knew I couldn't lie. I told him that I loved him as a best friend and nothing more. As I continued to reassure him that we could still be friends and nothing had to change, all I could see was his heart breaking right in front of me.

Nothing was the same after that night. We tiptoed around each other as agents for far too long. After a few years, I realized that being with the agency wasn't the right choice for me any longer. Truthfully, I'm not sure if it's because of what happened with Dodger or because I simply changed with age.

The allure of going into private security was appealing compared to working for the government. After I made my decision, I resigned and opened up my own firm.

As for Dodger, a few years ago, he was promoted to director of the agency. Now here we are playing a game of chess with each other. All moves between us are necessary and calculated.

Dodger knows I'm the best at what I do, and that's why he still calls me for special missions. The call we're about to have today is definitely a unique case that requires a specific skill set.

There's been a high volume of activity associated with the Marlin, and he needs me on the case now more than ever. The Marlin is one of the topmost criminals wanted by the agency, and this person's criminal activity has been getting worse with each passing day.

It began with whisperings that someone was trying to combine various mafia organizations across the country. Then, on a different case, I stumbled across confirmation that it was true.

The case I was working involved one of my top targets—the Kingpin of Charlotte. I'm convinced that the Kingpin of

Charlotte is connected to the Marlin. That's why I'm eager to tell him that I'll work with the agency to capture both of them. The Kingpin of Charlotte is the Marlin's primary connection to rare diamonds, and the Marlin uses these diamonds in trade to navigate the legal system undetected.

I've been tracking the Kingpin for over a year now, and he always manages to outsmart me. It's incredibly frustrating knowing that he's one step ahead. That's why, this time, I have a plan, one that took weeks to devise, knowing this call from Dodger was coming.

I plan to infiltrate the Carolinas mafia and pretend to be one of its own. I haven't attempted this yet because of the risk involved and the need for financial backing to do it right. By partnering with the agency on this, I'll be provided with the money needed to make it happen. My success rate as a contractor for them is nearly perfect.

LOGGING INTO THE VIDEO CALL, I'm a few minutes early to ensure I'm on ahead of Dodger. He's always been punctual.

As expected, it's eleven a.m. on the dot, and he's joining the call.

"Collins, thanks for joining me," he starts.

"Of course."

It's all formalities from my former friend.

"I'll get right to it—we need to hire you for an upcoming case. It'll be a new contract specific to this case only."

Meaning I can request whatever support and resources I'll need.

"The Marlin."

Dodger clears his throat and nods in confirmation.

"We need you to catch the Marlin. We have no idea who it is, and the illegal trade wars are off the charts. It's time to step in."

Interesting. They still have no known facts about any characteristics that would help identify the Marlin, similar to my situation with the Kingpin.

"I have a few leads regarding the Kingpin of Charlotte."

"The one who has ties to all of the Carolinas?"

"Yes."

"Very good."

There's an awkward pause.

"I know that's a tough one for you," he finishes.

Oh. My troubles capturing the Kingpin have spread through the grapevine.

"I have a plan. It's detailed and expensive and will require resources from the agency. I know I can capture them."

"Very good. I have one condition."

"What's that?"

"We're bringing on a partner for you to work with."

I twitch my lips, shocked.

"Excuse me? Dodger..."

I give him a tight smile to try and regroup internally without showing my disdain for the idea of working directly with a partner.

"Director, you know I work alone on my contracts."

Dodger drops the professional mask he's wearing and dramatically sighs. I'm not sure if it's out of annoyance or exhaustion.

"It's dangerous out there with the Marlin on the loose. The Kingpin of Charlotte is one of many we need to catch. This is bigger than your pride."

My head rears back as our walls come crumbling down. We haven't spoken like this in years.

"It's not pride; it's my work style. And aren't you the one who needs *my* help?"

Dodger raises his eyebrows, and a hint of a smile appears at the corner of his lips.

"Always the lone ranger."

"I work best alone."

He closes his eyes for a moment before sitting upright. His walls are back up, and I'm once again talking to the director and not my former friend.

"You'll take a partner, or I'll ask someone else."

He has me cornered, but I need this contract to fulfill my plans. I want to capture the Kingpin more than anything I've ever wanted from a contract.

I try to reason with myself about the idea of having a partner. I mean, really, how bad can a partner be? If anything, maybe it'll be better for me to infiltrate the Kingpin's domain if I have someone by my side in some capacity.

Wait. Wait a second...

"You have someone in mind."

"I do. Someone who is an expert in the field too. And this contractor has direct ties to Charlotte and the Carolinas area, which can only help you. He'll be an asset to your plans."

"He?" I ask.

"Yes. I have an idea of what you're thinking, and he will help you achieve your goal."

I have no choice. I either forfeit my best chance at capturing the Kingpin or work with this partner.

"I'll trust you."

"Good."

Dodger's surprised I'm giving in so easily, but what choice do I have? I need this win badly.

"I'll see you both in my office Wednesday at 0800 hours."

I nod curtly.

"Wednesday, Collins."

Dodger leaves the video call, and I'm feeling better than expected. I'm getting what I wanted out of this. Yes, I didn't expect a partner, but I'll take the lead, and everything will be just fine.

Twirling a pen in between my fingers, I start to think through how a partner can help my plans. Dodger might think he knows what my plans are, but there's no way he can understand the details I've put into this.

Anything he or this partner comes up with won't compare to what I have in store to capture the Marlin and bring down the Carolinas mafia.

"Ms. Collins?" Ruby's intercom sounds through my office. Reaching over to my corresponding machine, I press the button to speak.

"Come in."

Ruby enters a moment later and waits near the open doorway.

"We got it. I meet the director in two days," I share.

"That's great news!"

"It is. There's only one problem."

"What's that?"

"He has someone he wants me to partner with on it."

Ruby's eyebrows shoot up, and her mouth parts in disbelief.

"Believe me, I know. But I need this one. You know how much this means to me."

"I'll let you get to work then; I'll go ahead and get your look ready for tomorrow night."

"Thank you," I say, relieved.

Ruby gives me a small smile before leaving once again, probably thinking the same thing I am—I'm not exactly partner material, but this is something I don't have a choice on. I have to do this.

Alone once again, I start researching the latest news on organized crime activity in the Carolinas area. There may be a Kingpin of Charlotte, but the entire network is vast and complicated.

As I start going through the latest news, there's one article that catches my attention. A low-stakes robbery where the thief was arrested inside the jewelry store. When the cops apprehended him, there were no jewels to be found. He was ultimately arrested for breaking and entering and for resisting arrest, but not theft.

This has the Kingpin written all over it. Now my only question is, what exactly is he sending his foot soldiers out in search of? A robbery with no theft is beyond suspicious.

I add this to my digital crime board I've been compiling on the Kingpin.

Every day, there's something new, which makes me even hungrier to get to Charlotte and put my plans in motion. I've been on enough wild-goose chases to know that I'm closer than I've ever been before.

MY CELL PHONE vibrates on my desk, jolting me upright. I've been down this rabbit hole for so long that I hadn't even realized how much time had passed.

I take a sip of my lukewarm coffee as I pick up my phone. Flashing brightly is "Mom."

I groan, knowing my dad put her up to this. He's having my mother call me about the gala tomorrow night.

Even though I'm a single, thirty-six-year-old woman, my parents still insist that I attend their galas whenever I can. And while my work takes me away from California frequently, there are only so many times I can tell them no.

I'd rather avoid them all, but since I'm close with my parents, I attend for them. That's why I'm playing nice and going tomorrow.

"Hi," I say into the phone.

"Cara, sweetheart, it's been ages."

I roll my eyes and smile.

"Mom, I talked to you two days ago and the day before that."

"Well, it wasn't *yesterday*."

I giggle as I adjust the phone in my hand, knowing that I'm not going to keep arguing.

"Sweetie, we never talked about whether you are a definite yes for tomorrow night."

"I am," I relent.

"Oh good! Your father is going to be so happy to hear that."

"I'm sure he will be."

"Cara..." she sternly warns.

"What? Why does he go through you about this? Every. Single. Time."

"Hush now. Your father is a busy man who wears his heart on his sleeve for his girls."

I sit back in my chair and cross one of my legs over the other.

"And need I remind you, you getting into school in California and deciding to stay for all this security business is why we have a house out here too."

A hint of a smile touches my lips.

"I do."

"Good," she answers happily.

An alert pops up on my computer—a security issue notification.

"Sorry, Mom. I have to run. See you tomorrow. Love you."

"Love you too."

I check the alert and see my spyware has flagged the issue. All I need right now is for someone to break into my security measures ahead of prepping for this mission.

As I start to look at my computer screen, my attention is caught by the picture sitting on my desk of my parents and me.

We're on the beach together, in front of our favorite restaurant here in California. I can't help but feel happy staring at it.

Mom is right. My parents are the best that I could have gotten, and my dad runs his company from both coasts because of me.

They decided to move from my small Massachusetts hometown, Hull, out to California to be closer to me after college. My dad's company can be run from anywhere, so he has two locations.

Although they started being bicoastal for me, they enjoy going back and forth between the two coasts. It's almost all fun for them these days. That's why their second home is in Florida and not my hometown.

I know I'm lucky to be this close to them, but sometimes I wonder what it would have been like if I weren't an only child. Many of the decisions they made over the years revolved around me. It's partially why I can be guilted into activities such as attending a gala with people I can't stand to be around.

I wince at an intrusive thought.

There may be one person in particular I don't want to see. One person I'm always dreading running into at these social gatherings.

I know he will be there; he always is.

I sigh.

Grant Sinclair is always everywhere.

STARING OUT MY LARGE WINDOWS, I'm in awe of the view. The sun setting and casting a glimmering shine on the ocean will never get old. Living on the beach has always been a dream of mine.

When I entered the private sector, I was able to earn more money from one contract alone than I would have earned in an entire year working for the agency.

Dodger couldn't believe that I was willing to "sell my soul for a better paycheck," but here we are. With each passing day, any memory that I have of Dodger only highlights our differences. I'm not sure our friendship would have lasted regardless of the situation we found ourselves in.

"This is stunning. Seriously, Cara, you look beautiful in this dress." Ruby beams from the other side of my living room.

"It's Cara now, is it?" I tease.

"Okay, fine, Ms. Collins. You are gorgeous," she retorts playfully.

In the office, Ruby and I like to keep our relationship professional; we're women in the security field, and there are already enough hurdles we have to jump over on a daily basis.

"You think so?"

"Yes, this sparkling black is phenomenal. Good thing you have an assistant with excellent taste shopping for you."

"Thank you, Ruby," I singsong.

It's true; I don't know what I'd do without her taking care of so many aspects of my personal life.

Ruby looks down at her cell phone and back up at me.

"Your car service is here."

"Already?"

"Right on time, just how you like it."

"I'll just add my jewelry, then I'll be ready to go."

"It's in your bedroom."

"Can you ask the driver to wait?"

"On it."

I smile and head back into my bedroom, where I immediately spot the two jewelry boxes. Quickly, I put my black diamond stud earrings in first and then add the thin coordinating black diamond necklace.

As I stare at myself in my mirror, I can't help but feel content. Some might get lonely living this life, but not me. Sometimes I think about what it would be like to have a life partner by my side, but then I'm reminded that if something goes wrong at work, that could never be possible.

Plus, I am happy. I have a good support system around me and enjoy my career. It doesn't need to be perfect to be right.

Time to get it together and head to this gala. Focusing back on my reflection, I tighten my stomach and pull back my shoulders.

I'm Cara Collins, and I've captured hundreds of criminals. The Kingpin of Charlotte is within my grasp. I know it's going to happen. I can handle one night seeing Grant Sinclair.

Feeling confident, I go to add the final touch to my outfit. I hike up my dress, strap my gun to my upper thigh, and slip a small knife in between my breasts.

This may be a charity gala, but I'm always prepared for any unexpected issues.

Heading back out to Ruby, I grab my clutch and double-check it has all the essentials.

"Your car will be ready to pick you up as soon as you call the number on the card in your purse."

I cock an eyebrow.

"Don't look at me like that. You know your one-hour rule changes when you're with your parents."

I grin, and she gives me a teasing look back.

"Fine. I'll text the number this time."

"And is there anything else outstanding that you need me to finish on your presentation?"

"If you can just give it a final once over, that would be great. I want it to be perfect for the meeting."

"Will do. I'll send you a final file tonight."

"Thank you."

"Now go stun the ballroom."

"It's now or never."

I head out down the pathway from my front door, ready to take on the evening.

"Oh, and *Ms. Collins*?"

"Yes?" I ask while looking over my shoulder.

"Don't go killing your future husband tonight."

I smirk.

"No promises."

TWO

Grant

"THIS IS GRANT."

"Grant, it's been a while," Dodger says from the other line.

"Not since Reno."

"Right, Reno. The Masked... What were we calling that one?"

"The Masked Millionaire."

"That's it. All the money in the world, and he still went and stole more from his friends."

My driver slows to a stop at the flashing four-way stop. The engine roars to life, making me miss whatever small talk Dodger is continuing with.

"What do you say?" he asks.

"Missed it."

Dodger clears his throat, obviously frustrated that I wasn't giving him my full attention.

We have an interesting relationship, to say the least. He

hates using me for contract work. There's never been an incident to my knowledge, but what do I know? I usually stick to myself in this line of work. My personal life gives me enough opportunities to experience connection, so I don't need to become friends with anyone out in the field.

I tuned Dodger out again.

"Sorry, mate. It's this reception out toward the sea. You understand."

"I have a contract. I'm going for the Marlin, and it requires a partner. She'll have a plan already in place," he answers angrily.

"She?"

"She's the best in the field. You'll get along well."

"What time? Where?"

"Tomorrow. My office. 0800 hours."

"See you then."

I hang up and slip my cell phone inside my tuxedo jacket pocket.

"Almost there, boss," my driver calls out.

"Thanks."

My driver has been with me for years, which I'm grateful for. He knows what I do and often supports me in my endeavors outside of driving me to events for personal and professional reasons.

"Confirming, pick you up in an hour?"

"Not tonight. I'll be in touch."

"Aha."

"Don't comment." I sigh.

"Not me. Never, sir."

This is his sign that she'll be there—Cara. My best friend's daughter, my rival, and sadly, the most beautiful woman I've ever laid eyes on. It's quite the situation I've found myself in.

I still remember the first time that we discovered we were both in this line of work. The night that Dodger hedged his bets and hired two contractors for the same case in addition to the slew of agents he had working on it already.

The night we caught the Masked Millionaire.

A WOMAN. *A woman beat me to him.*

I wouldn't call myself a sexist man. In fact, I love women. Women can be in any field. I know of some agents and even a few other contractors who are great at this job. My issue is I've never had one beat me to a capture before. Honestly, I can't even remember the last man who beat me to a victory.

Long, pitch-black hair is high in a ponytail, swinging against her thin yet strong frame. She's wearing all black since its best to blend in with the night.

The way her leather pants are shaping against her ass is mouthwatering. I usually get a twitch in my cock when I capture my conquest, but this is entirely new.

The wanted man is tied to a chair with a gag in his mouth—or so I assume from the muffled sounds coming from the opposite side of the warehouse.

The woman flips a gun with one hand and props the other on her hip. The way her heels elongate her already mile-long legs isn't helping me stay focused.

There's only one woman this could be.

She's kept her identity mostly hidden from me. I'm sure I could have figured it out by now, but I've never had a reason to.

I've followed her career, and it's been impressive, including a near-perfect record of contracts she's taken.

I methodically step forward to see her work in person. She freezes in place, clearly not expecting anyone else to have found the Masked Millionaire's hideout as quickly as she did.

Part of me wants to taunt her, and I'm not sure where this urge is really coming from.

I start to give a slow clap as I continue my approach.

"Well done."

Her shoulders straighten, and her back goes rigid.

"Are you with him?" she asks.

The way her voice feels like velvet as her words roll off her tongue only intensifies my need to taunt this woman.

I laugh darkly as I slip my hands in my pockets.

"I don't think so, darling."

"I'm not your darling, sweetheart."

A silent laugh vibrates along the length of her body as the Masked Millionaire's muffled sounds continues. The rocking of the wooden chair he's tied to bangs against the cement floor as he struggles in the ropes.

"Nice knot work," I say.

"It's perfect."

A perfectionist. I can appreciate that.

"Looks like our dear friend, the director, hired us both to find him," I say.

I'm almost flush against her back, needing her to say anything in return. The way her floral scent wafts through the air makes me crave this woman even more.

"What's your plan here? You've got him. What else do you need?" I rasp.

"I need a piece of information."

"What's that?"

She laughs warmly, and in this moment, I know I'm utterly fucked.

"I'll never tell."

"Come on, darling. Tell me what you need."

"I don't think so."

"Let's start fresh here. My friends call me Ace, and you must be... my lucky charm."

Her whimsical laughter fills the warehouse, and it's the only sound I ever want to hear.

"I'll never be your anything."

She spins around and props a hand back on her hip. As I study this woman's face, a shocked expression crosses it.

Realization dawns on me moments later.

"Car—" I start, and she puts a hand over my mouth immediately.

"Fuck," she mutters.

I almost blew her cover in front of this criminal she's torturing.

"You?" I ask, shocked.

"And you."

"We have to talk."

"After."

I pinch my eyebrows together in disbelief.

"What do you need from him?"

"I'll get it myself. Go. Please."

"Fuck. You can have this one," I relent.

This is not good.

"Meet me at Willow Park in two hours."

"Two hours," she confirms.

I exit through a side set of dingy doors and leave her to it.

Two hours later, I find myself in Willow Park waiting. An hour passes by, and I realize Cara isn't coming.

If this is how she wants to play it, then that's fine by me.

Game on, Cara Collins.

"WE'RE HERE, SIR."

"Thank you."

My driver opens my door, and I step out of the black SUV. This gala is thrown annually by my best friend, Luke, and his wife, Catherine.

We met when he moved to California, and I was assisting with a business deal. As a businessman, I dabble in real estate and other ventures, anything to boost my portfolio. That's why a friend asked for a favor—to help him make a deal with Collins Enterprises and his corporation.

Luke is tough as nails when it comes to negotiation. After several days, we finally came to an agreement and decided to celebrate.

We went out for a few cocktails and got along better than anyone I had previously met in California. That's when I knew he was someone I'd be friends with for years to come.

Not only is he a good businessman, but he's also proud of what he's accomplished with his family. That day, he told me every decision he made was to better his family's future and not for his own egotistical gains. After I heard that, I took him under my wing, and the rest is history.

I met Cara only once before the night of the Masked Millionaire.

It all made sense after that discovery. We both were consistently invited to her parents' galas and parties, but given our mutual profession, our paths rarely crossed.

I thought she was breathtaking that night we met but clearly off-limits given my relationship with her father.

Now tonight is another one that I have to spend looking at the most beautiful woman I know, who is out of reach.

As I walk up the museum steps, I spot my old friends right away. Catherine sees me as they greet guests entering the building and slightly nudges Luke. As I get into the back of the line, Luke waves me forward to skip ahead.

Passing by the guests, I can't help but scan for any sign of Cara. Of course she wouldn't be in the actual line, but I'm pathetic when it comes to getting a sighting of this woman. She may be untouchable, but I can still appreciate the effect she has on me.

She's here. I can feel her presence, but I wouldn't expect her to be in line with her parents. Instead, I know she's keeping to the shadows and watching everyone from a distance.

I'll find her; I always do as she's come to learn.

"Luke," I say, greeting him with a hug.

"Grant. I'm glad you were able to make it. All my favorite people are able to be here tonight. It's wonderful."

"Happy to support."

"Grant." Catherine greets me with a hug as well.

"Another beautiful event," I answer.

"That's sweet of you. Why don't you two go get a drink? I've got this covered."

"If you insist, dear," Luke answers. He places a chaste kiss on her cheek that she leans into.

"Ready?" Luke asks. I chuckle with a shake of my head.

"I see the bar calling our name."

"How's business?" he asks as we walk inside.

"Good. Busy. You know how traveling is these days."

"It's exhausting work. That's why I'm glad that we decided to settle here and keep a home on both coasts. No need for rentals or hotel rooms."

"You have the life, old friend."

"That I do," he says with pride.

Luke flags down the bartender and orders us two bourbons neat. The bartender quickly pours the amber liquid and slides them in front of us. We take the glasses and clink them together.

"To friendship," he says.

I give him a curt nod, and we both take a sip.

"Anything new on your end?" I ask.

He sighs, and a sense of sadness flickers across his face.

"What is it?"

"It's nothing."

"I can see that's not true."

"Just getting old. I'm not as young as you are," he says playfully.

"You're not that much older, *old man*."

He laughs and takes another sip of his drink.

"Ten years makes a difference at this age. I was hoping to have a successor to my company by now, but you know how Cara is. She has her own life."

"You're inching closer to sixty. You have time to find one."

"I hope that's true."

"And you know any help I can give you, just say the word."

"I may take you up on that. Selling at some point down the road seems like the most suitable answer. It would just have to be to the right person."

I can tell my friend is worried about what the future holds. I give him a pat on the shoulder and hold on tight for a moment.

"Let's stop this nonsense for tonight. It's a party," Luke says.

"Down the hatch then, *old man*."

He smirks as we both finish our drinks and flag down the bartender for another round.

"I'll take one of those too, please," a sultry voice says.

Cara's nails graze lightly against the back of my jacket.

"Dad," she says while removing her hand.

The feeling of her touch lingers—an unavoidable buzz of electricity every time she touches me in some way. It happens so rarely that I soak it in every time.

Cara gives Luke a hug and, as she pulls away, gestures to the bartender for that drink.

"Grant."

"Cara."

We lean in toward one another, and I let my hand graze her lower back as I pull her closer to my side. Placing a gentle kiss on her cheek, I hear the faint sound of her breath hitching.

She peers up at me, and I see a flicker of desire in her deep-brown eyes.

"How are you, darling?" I whisper into her ear.

As I pull away, I see the same hint of annoyance that I've come to crave during our challenges. Cara hates to lose, and I love to capture the criminal before she does just to earn this look.

"Just as charming as always, Sinclair."

"I should be the one to say that, Collins."

We're having a stare-down, and Luke's eyes dart between the two of us.

"What's this about?"

Cara breaks eye contact first and smiles at her father.

"Nothing at all."

Luke will accept it, but I can admit we both let the

moment get the best of us when we referred to each other by our government names.

"I'm happy you were able to come," he says to Cara.

"Me too, Dad. I'm not sure if I'll be around for a bit."

"Oh? Why is that?"

"A new work project. I think it'll take me away for a few months."

I wonder what case she's on. I'll be sure to have someone at my firm find out tomorrow. It must be big if it'll be a few months. Typically, contracts don't take you away for that long. Cara is both daring and cautious, so I know she'll have thought this through.

It'll just irk me until I'm able to figure out what the case is exactly and how safe she'll be.

"Just don't tell your mother tonight," Luke says.

"I won't, but I'll have to this week."

"Okay, try to come by the house before you go."

"Luke!" Catherine calls out from nearby.

We all look to see Catherine standing with some of their gala's top donors. It's a good cause that they host this to support every year, so the top donors tend to be the same people year after year.

"Duty calls. Play nice, you two," he says.

"Always," Cara answers.

Luke gives us a warm smile before heading to Catherine. As he walks away, the bartender slides Cara's and my fresh bourbons over. She picks hers up and gives me a mocking look.

I can't help but drink *her* in.

She is a vision. The way this dress hugs her curves perfectly is dangerous, and her natural chestnut-brown hair hanging against her breasts has my cock twitching in my pants.

I hope she doesn't see it.

She smirks as I meet her eyes.

"Can you make it any more obvious?" she taunts before taking a sip of the drink.

"You're a gorgeous woman. I won't deny that."

She cocks an eyebrow as she lets the rim of her glass linger against her dark-red painted lips.

"But?" she finally asks.

"It's a shame the package comes with all this damn sass."

A wide grin spreads across her face, and I can't help but let my teasing smirk grow too.

"Don't worry, sweetheart. I have no issues finding real men who can handle it all."

Cara downs the rest of her bourbon and slams it on the bar.

"See you out there," she says, flipping her long hair over her shoulder as she walks away.

This woman always has to have the last word. Why did I freeze when she responded? It can't be the feeling of jealousy working its way through my system.

Cara can be with other men; it's not like I'm a saint. And it's not like I can have the woman—there would be too many obstacles in our way.

For one, I'm getting old. I may not be Luke's age, but the wear and tear I've put on my body with decades of field experience makes me feel like I am.

When I was first starting out, the adventure, the travel, and hell, even the women all played into why I loved this constant game I still find myself in. There was too much appeal for a young hotshot to say no.

Nowadays, the lure to retire is constantly on my mind. I'm not sure what it'll take to make me finally lay my superhero complex to rest, but it'll happen one day soon. Until then, I've been setting myself up nicely in the background. Having connections from around the world has put me in a good financial position. If I do ever manage to say goodbye to this life, I'll be able to work my other businesses with ease.

I sip my bourbon and swirl the remainder around in the glass. Cara's laughing at some young man across the room. The sound of her laughter ringing in the distance is almost intoxicating. *Almost.*

I don't even have to know what they're talking about to understand he serves a purpose to her; otherwise, she wouldn't be wasting her time. It's all a façade she's putting on with him to get under my skin.

I track the way Cara's hand rests on the man's forearm, making him relax despite the fact that she's leading the conversation between the two of them.

He leans close to her ear, and she pulls back playfully before putting her hand in his. She pauses before he can pull her out onto the dance floor, and I see a slight shiver race up her spine.

Cara slowly glances in my direction. She can sense my presence. It's this vulnerable version of her that makes me forget about all the complications that make Cara Collins.

She knew I was watching. More importantly, she *liked it.*

Cara grins before focusing back on her dance partner. He whisks her out of my line of sight, probably for the best.

I have two options here.

The first is to simply get another drink, find Luke and Catherine, and maybe find a woman of my own for the night. The problem is that this irking feeling won't go away. This leads me to option two: go out there and steal the girl.

"Really, darling. I'm at a loss."

"Don't *darling* me," she snarls and tries to get out of my hold.

"Cara. Don't. Really, I don't know what you're talking about," I plead.

I like to mess with her more than anyone, but I'd never intentionally steal a contract.

"Don't do that to me," she whispers.

"Cara. What contract?"

"The Holden Company. I was meant to handle their new security setup, but lo and behold, I find out that Grant Sinclair is starting on it."

I let go of her waist and take a step back.

"They came to me. It was a normal transaction. I had one of my guys press for competitors, and they said there were none. You know that was just business."

"Business," she says slowly.

"Yes, it happens. You can't hold me personally accountable."

She smiles as she straightens her back.

"You're right. I can't hold you accountable. You wouldn't know the first thing about someone getting close enough to you and wanting to do right by them."

Cara spins on her heels and walks away.

This time, I let her. If I know anything at all, it's that I'll be seeing her sooner than she wants. That's how it's always been between the two of us.

THREE

Cara

I STRAIGHTEN the strap of my brown leather briefcase against my shoulder and look into the mirrored elevator doors at the agency.

I'm ready.

After a terrible night facing Grant the day after I had learned he stole the Holden contract right out from under me, I need this to go well to get my boost of confidence back. When I returned home from the gala, I focused on reviewing the updated plans I'll be sharing with Dodger and my new partner today.

I can't believe that Grant is pretending like they didn't tell him I was their other choice. It is business, but this one was personal.

Grant can pretend like he doesn't remember all he wants, but the Holden Company is the one I've wanted since I went private.

I'll never forget how one of their leaders said security couldn't be run by a woman. They rejected me for a different company led by a man, and I vowed that I would one day get another one of their contracts and exceed their expectations just to prove a point.

Grant knows about my past with the Holden Company. I told him when we were both hiding out in Barcelona after a shoot-out we found ourselves in. I was off my game, and he noticed. There were no jabs or sparring between us; instead, he listened to me for hours.

When I told him what happened, he gave me some advice I still hold onto.

It was one of the rare moments when we weren't competing in the field or forced together because of my parents. It was raw and real… and unforgettable.

That's why I hate that he took this opportunity from me.

I stretch my neck from side to side and tighten my stomach, waiting for the elevator doors to open. Taking a deep breath, I close my eyes and try to focus on the mission ahead and not Grant Sinclair.

"Collins," a familiar voice rasps.

Oh no.

I peel one eye open, followed by the next, and take another steadying breath.

"Sinclair."

I can feel heat exuding off him as he stands entirely too close behind me. If I were to lean back, I could do some damage by elbowing him in the stomach.

I grin at the idea.

Pity I have some semblance of control, being at the agency and all.

"Take a step back, pretty boy."

A deep rumble faintly sounds.

"It's been a while since I've been called that."

"You're right. It was far too much of a compliment for my liking."

Another hint of laughter that I'm embarrassed to admit I enjoyed getting out of him.

"What will you call me instead?"

"Old man."

"Ouch," he says with a faint laugh.

"Call it like I see 'em."

The elevator doors open, and I walk in without looking back. As I turn around, I see he's coming in with me.

Just great.

"You know, I'm not that much older than you."

"Yes, you are."

He smiles as he takes his place next to me so we're both watching the elevator doors close. I press the button to the floor I need and resume my original position.

"Maybe," he offers.

I peer up at him and take in the graying hair and wrinkles gathering around his eyes.

"How old are you anyway?"

One side of his mouth tilts upward.

"Trying to get to know me after all these years?"

"You can keep your secrets."

"Forty-nine."

My eyes widen in surprise. Not at his age but at the notion that Grant so freely shared something truthful with me. That's not common in our business of lies and deception.

The elevator door dings and begins to open.

"You're right."

"What's that?" he asks as I straighten my suit jacket.

"It's not *that* much older than me."

I step off and don't give him a chance to say anything else.

As I walk toward Dodger's assistant, I hear footsteps behind me. I glance back to see Grant following slowly in the same direction.

Wait.

Wait just a second.

There is no one else on this floor other than Dodger.

"Is this the right floor for you?" I ask.

"It is."

"But my meeting with him is in ten minutes."

Grant finally steps right before me.

"Well, Cara. Looks like we're in the same meeting."

I hang my head back and hold the bridge of my nose.

"Fuck," I mutter.

"Indeed."

He walks past me as if this isn't our worst nightmare about to become a reality.

"Sinclair. Collins. Mr. Ross will be available shortly," the assistant calls out before we even have a chance to reach her.

"Thank you," we say in unison.

Grant gestures to the chairs in the waiting area.

I take a seat, and he takes the one opposite me on the other side of the room.

Placing my briefcase in my lap, I cross my legs together at the ankles.

This cannot be happening.

There's no way Dodger knows about Grant's and my

complicated history. Otherwise, he wouldn't have asked us to work together in this capacity.

There's no way that Grant and I can work together on this contract.

I let out a deep, steadying breath.

Okay, Cara, think this through.

The problem is that if I tell him I don't want to work with Grant, there is a high probability that he will take me off this case instead of Grant. I can't let that happen.

I've been chasing after the Kingpin of Charlotte for a year now. Grant knows this too. He's been on my heels when I've received new information regarding the Kingpin's activities.

Despite Dodger knowing that I have all this intel, Grant is the best of the best. I would never admit that to him, but it's true, which is probably why Dodger put us together.

"I'm not going to turn this down, Collins."

My eyes snap up to Grant's, and I see the conviction behind them.

"I'm not either."

"Good."

We're in a battle of wills as we continue our stare-off.

"Mr. Ross will see you now," his assistant says, interrupting us.

I look up to see she's standing and waiting for us to notice that she's there. She gives me a curt nod before heading into Dodger's office.

Grant and I stand at the same time, and he gestures for me to go on ahead. It's infuriating how a simple gesture from him can get under my skin like this.

As I walk into Dodger's office, I know I have to be confident and ready, regardless of whether the mission now involves my archnemesis.

I can do this.

I'm a professional.

I won't let Grant Sinclair ruin me.

"SINCLAIR. COLLINS. TAKE A SEAT," Dodger says.

He's tapping away at his computer with a stern expression. It's the same one I would see on him every day after we both joined the agency. An unsettling feeling washes over.

He won't look up at us as we take the two empty seats in his sterile office. As I scan his desk, there's no sign of life. No pictures of friends or family, no decorative objects, and I mean, come on, there isn't even a plant.

My gaze catches on Grant's, who has also been assessing the office. He gives me a slight tilt of the head before focusing back on Dodger.

Dodger's shoulders are tense as he pauses his fingers on the keys. Only a few moments pass before he resumes his work again.

I straighten my posture with my bag in my lap, gripping the strap as a distraction. I don't normally feel like this when it comes to meetings, but this is unlike any meeting I've been part of in a while.

First, Grant surprises me by being here, and now this tactic by Dodger is baffling. Something isn't normal, and I'm anxious to find out what that may be.

Dodger finally stops his typing and settles back into his worn brown chair. He grips the ends of the armrests as he stares at Grant and me.

"Thank you both for being here today."

"Of course," I answer first.

Grant gives a slight nod.

"Well, I'll get right to it. The agency needs you two so we can get the Marlin."

"What information do you have for us? You know my work has focused on the Kingpin of Charlotte and surrounding areas."

"That's why you two are together."

I briefly study Grant's face, and I realize he knows more about the Marlin than I do. His expression is tense as he waits for Dodger to continue.

"Can you bring me up to speed?" I ask.

"The Marlin is the code name for the head of the underground ring we've been trying to infiltrate for years. As you may or may not know, there have never been any defining details about the person to come to light. You both have ties to the Marlin, which is why I've brought you both on."

"Right, but we knew that. Do you think that the Marlin is with the Kingpin of Charlotte?"

"Yes," Grant answers before Dodger can.

My head shakes at how this meeting has evolved in mere minutes.

"Collins, your information and search to date on the Kingpin of Charlotte have been our primary connection to the Marlin until now."

Dodger straightens his tie as I look at him, utterly confused.

"What is it?" I ask.

Grant remains silent next to me, almost as if none of this is new information for him.

"We have reason to believe that the Marlin is in hiding in Charlotte at this very moment. Due to this, Collins, I'm asking you to go and infiltrate their organization and capture the Marlin."

"Sir. With all due respect," I start.

"Don't, Collins. Do you want this one or not?" Dodger asks.

"I do."

"Then it's settled. You're going. And Sinclair is going with you."

"I don't understand his connection to this," I admit.

Grant finally adjusts in his seat.

"I've known about the Marlin for a while."

"What?" I shout.

"The Marlin will know of me as Ace."

"Ace," I repeat.

The same code name he gave me that first night we discovered each other in the field.

"Collins. Sinclair. Your new identities and details will be waiting outside with my assistant."

"Sir," I continue.

Dodger sighs.

"Collins. Are you in or not? I can't keep asking."

"You haven't even asked our friend Ace here if he's in."

Dodger gives me an annoyed look before glancing over to Grant.

"I'm in. When do we leave?"

"Wheels up in three days at 0600 hours from San Diego."

Dodger looks back over at me.

"I'm in."

"Good. Mr. and Mrs. Weston, good luck."

I nearly faint on the spot.

"Did you say..."

"Come on, Collins," Grant says as he stands.

I look up at his outstretched hand, feeling like I'm in some kind of other universe. I can't marry Grant, even if it is all pretend.

"What about my *plans*?" I ask Dodger.

He glances up at me, and I see my weathered friend feels for what I'm about to go through despite his lack of knowledge about my relationship with Grant.

"You're lead on this, Collins. Share any plans with your new partner."

Slowly, my fallen façade reappears. Standing up, I pull my jacket around me tightly and shift my briefcase bag around my shoulder.

"Will do, sir."

With my mask in place, I stoically march out of Dodger's office with Grant on my heels.

I walk toward Dodger's assistant, and she's standing in front of her desk with two sealed packets in her hands. As I approach, she silently hands one to me and then one to Grant.

He follows me as I leave, and we reach the elevator silently.

As I enter, I press the first-floor button and watch as the doors close with us both inside.

"You need to do better," he says.

I flinch and slowly turn to look up at his two hazel eyes.

"Excuse me?" I ask slowly.

"You're better than that. Don't let Dodger get to you."

"I was professional."

"You were emotional."

My head rears back in astonishment before I face forward once again.

"You're better than that."

"You don't even know me, Sinclair. Despite what you may think, you have no idea who I am or how I work."

"Cara."

"Don't call me that."

"I know you're one of the best contractors out there. I know you have one of the top five sniper shots in the world."

Grant pauses, and I feel the warmth of his breath lightly touching the shell of my ear. It causes goose bumps to prick along my skin.

I turn around and face him once more. When I do, our faces are mere inches away from one another.

One thing I hate the most about Grant Sinclair is that he is every bit as breathtaking as the reputation that precedes him. I want to say he's not my type, but as I'm caught in his line of sight, I long to stay here.

"You're a phenomenal daughter who continually goes above and beyond for her parents. You value family. You value those who you let yourself get close to. You care more than anyone in our line of work should. You are Cara Collins. The best there is."

My mouth parts as I bask in his words.

"Don't let someone like Dodger get under your skin."

He waits for me to reply, but how can I respond to that? He just crossed every line we've ever put between us. All my mixed emotions about the man are swirling around my mind, making me feel lightheaded.

The elevator dings and begins to open, and we both automatically face the door. I readjust my bag on my shoulder and grin as I face him one last time.

"I think you'd like to be the only man who gets under my skin."

Grant grins widely back.

I step off the elevator and hear him behind me as we head to the double doors to leave the agency.

"Tomorrow, 0500 hours. Meet me at the Skyline Diner. We need to go over our plans."

"See you there, darling," he says with a faint laugh.

THE DINER IS my favorite one in the city. It's close to the agency and my office, but it's more than that. It reminds me of simpler times. Almost as if it has been frozen in a past era.

The owner is a wrinkled older man who still works the cash register and counter. His granddaughter handles the rest of the tables. It's usually relatively empty, but it really shouldn't be—they have the best cinnamon rolls in town.

I'm here before five in the morning, wanting to get settled in before Grant's arrival. His words from yesterday are still weighing heavily on my mind.

I was off-kilter when Dodger told me the latest news and updates. He wants me to pretend to be married to Grant to infiltrate the Carolinas mafia. It wasn't far from what I was originally thinking, but I never considered the possibility that my partner in this would be Grant Sinclair.

Capturing the Marlin will be one of my crowning moments in the field, more so than my conquest of the Kingpin. What I need is for Grant to allow me to take the lead on this so I can bring them all down together.

I'm not sure what to think after everything he said in the elevator.

I hate Grant Sinclair with every fiber of my being, yet his words penetrated me deeply like no one else has done before.

I take a sip of my black coffee. The jingle from the front door fills the diner, and I know it's going to be Grant. Glancing down at my watch, I see it's five a.m. on the dot. As expected, Grant is punctual, a trait he shares with my old friend, Dodger.

Grant scans the mostly empty diner and spots me immediately, giving me a small nod as he walks toward the red faux-leather booth I'm sitting in.

He slides into the opposite side as his camel trench coat molds to his body with his easy movements.

"Collins. Come here often?" he asks as he folds his hands on the table.

"I do."

Our server comes over right away and sets a coffee mug in front of Grant. He graciously accepts it and asks for a water as well.

"Caffeine and hydration," I comment.

"Important for this hour."

"Did I get you out of bed too early? Sorry if I'm messing with your beauty sleep."

He smirks as he pours a creamer pod into his coffee.

"For you? I'll get up at four a.m. and head across town any day."

"Right." I scoff.

I readjust in my seat and pull out a folder I made for Grant. It has more details than the one we were both given by the agency.

Sliding it over, he stops it in the middle of the table.

"Collins. I have no doubt that you've laid out everything as is, but I think we need to have a conversation before diving into the Carolinas mafia."

"I agree." I sigh.

"I know this organization," he starts.

I go to interrupt, but he puts his hand up slightly.

"I know you do too. But it's different for me. I'll explain everything eventually."

"But?"

"But I know them. Well. Not from afar."

I breathe out a long wind of air.

"What are you saying?"

"If Dodger wants us to pretend to be married, then we have to commit."

I glance around the room to buy time. What is he saying? Sensing my confusion, Grant runs his hand down his face. He looks pained to have to explain this to me.

"Collins. We need to get married."

"What?" I practically shout.

"Yes."

"Why? We aren't going in as Cara Collins and Grant Sinclair. Why would we have to get married?"

"We need the paperwork. We can get it forged. I know a guy locally. But we have to get a marriage certificate. They'll look into us if I'm coming back into the fold."

"Okay, right, our aliases have to get married. Not actually *us*."

"No, but..."

He stretches in the booth, and I take it as a stall tactic to gather his thoughts. It'll be important to know his tells if we're doing this for the next few months.

"I think we should get married in case things go poorly. We can't testify against one another. Legally."

"If things go poorly? Sinclair."

I shut my eyes tightly before opening and looking up at him.

He looks tired, not because of the early hour but because of what this situation entails. It finally hits me. This isn't just a contract for him either; Grant wants this just as much as I do.

"This operation will be the one that defines both of our careers. Despite our diverging interests most of the time, this one is different. We're on the same team. With that comes complications."

I lean back in the booth while weighing my options. Even though Grant Sinclair drives me crazy, I know deep down that he wouldn't intentionally want to be married to me unless it was crucial to do so.

"Alright, Grant. We'll do it your way. Let's get married."

FOUR

Grant

"GRANT? EVERYTHING ALRIGHT?" Luke asks.

I glance up at my friend, who's waiting for me to tee off at this hole. We've somehow managed to keep this golf tee time together for the past decade. Once a month, we try to meet to play a round and catch up.

These days, my line of work doesn't often interfere with it. I'm rarely gone for as long as I will be this time around.

"All good," I answer as I line up my shot.

"Where is it you're taking off to this time?"

"You know I can't tell you."

Luke chuckles behind me as I take my swing. The ball sails far, and we head into the golf cart to keep going.

"Always shrouded in mystery."

"Part of the gig."

I start to drive as Luke hangs on in the passenger seat.

"One day, you'll have to tell me what it is you do."

"One day, I'll be retired and able to share all my tales."

Luke grins as we slow down.

"Cara's heading out too."

He gets out of the cart and starts to go for a golf club before pausing.

Luke shakes his head, almost as if he's talking himself out of whatever thought he was having. I grab my next club, too, and follow him toward the fairway.

One secret that I keep for Cara, out of professional courtesy, is that I don't tell her father anything about our overlapping lines of work. He knows she does something in security but has no idea what his daughter is capable of. It's for his safety that he can't know what our cases involve.

We both take our shots and find ourselves at the hole, putting the balls in.

"I'm about ready for the 19th hole," Luke jokes as he picks up the ball.

"Almost there. Only two more holes left."

"You'll be able to do a couple of drinks?"

"Wouldn't miss it."

"Good," Luke answers.

"Just remember, I'm beating you out here," I tease.

"You always do."

We head to the next hole and find ourselves in a familiar position.

"Come on, old man. Show me what you've got."

Luke gets more serious as he focuses on the ball and prepares to take his shot.

I do have an ulterior motive for making sure he and I were able to get together before Cara and I leave for Charlotte. I'm about to marry his daughter, and he has no idea that, on paper, I'm going to be his son-in-law. Before I marry Cara, I want a bit of insight into her before making her my wife. All for educational reasons, of course.

"YOU WIN AGAIN," Luke says with a sigh.

In the club's restaurant, we both look at the drink menu as we wait for a server to come by and take our orders.

"It happens from time to time," I tease.

"If I were ten years younger like you."

"Then I'd be in real trouble."

A server comes by, and we place our order. The service is good at this club, so it doesn't take long for our cocktails to arrive.

Luke smiles as he takes a sip of his gin and tonic while I take a drink of my vodka martini. A bit cliché, but it's popular for a reason.

Luke lets out a long groan.

"Is everything good with you?"

"It is. Catherine is doing great. It's just Cara I worry about."

I snort in disbelief.

"You've raised a good one. Whatever she's up to, she'll be just fine."

He hums, but I see him wrestling inside.

"Her work is her life. It's a mystery, almost like yours," he says.

Luke takes another sip of his cocktail and places it back down on the table.

"But I worry about everything else she's sacrificing to chase this dream of hers. I'm not even sure if it's a dream or a nightmare she's trying to solve. She only shares so much, but I see the heaviness she carries."

Interesting.

"What is she sacrificing?"

"A family of her own."

"You want her to settle down?"

"If it's what she wants."

Another long sigh spills from Luke.

"The problem is that she's never brought anyone home to her mother and me because of this job, so I have no idea if she even wants a family. I don't even know if she knows herself."

I take a sip of my martini and wait for my friend to continue to vent. He scrubs a hand down his face.

"I'm proud of her. We both are. Even with how cryptic it all is."

"Good, as you should be."

"I just hope she knows what she's doing. Work can't be her entire life forever. Hell, you, of all people, have to understand where I'm coming from with that."

"You're right. I do."

Luke's expression twists into one of remorse.

"Sorry. I didn't mean it like that."

"No, you're right. I was Cara in my thirties and now my forties too. I've never settled down. Always chasing the next big adventure."

"I just want her to be happy, and I wonder if she is."

I wonder that, too, but I won't admit that to him.

"Who do you think would be right for Cara as a partner?"

Luke studies me for a moment, and his mouth twists as he debates his answer. For someone who wants his daughter to be settled down, clearly, he doesn't have anyone in mind.

"Well, I think what I do know is that the person has to be career-driven."

"That makes sense."

"Someone who won't let her walk all over them."

"Also, fair point."

"And... someone who can peel back her layers and see she's got the biggest damn heart of anyone I've ever met. She deserves someone who will be her equal and her partner. Someone who will show her she doesn't have to go at it all alone."

"She'll get that. One day. She will. I'm sure she wants that too."

"I hope so."

"Who do you think Cara would want?"

"Someone witty, with a sense of humor. Smart, has to be smart, or she would eat that person alive."

"Do you think she's attracted to men?"

"Yes."

"But you haven't seen her bring anyone home."

"No, but I see the types she gravitates toward. Cara wouldn't have an issue flirting with anyone at one of our parties. She knows Catherine and I would love to meet whoever she was with."

"Who is her type then?"

"Maybe tall," he starts and then laughs.

"What's funny?"

"Tall, dark, handsome, and older."

He lets out a hearty laugh.

"That's a good type to be."

"Funny, I basically described you."

Luke's cell phone vibrates on the table. He picks it up and answers immediately. It must be Catherine.

"Hey, sweetheart," he says.

He doesn't catch the way I've frozen from his earlier comment.

Luke holds up a finger to indicate he'll be right back and starts to leave our table. As he does, I settle into my chair.

I know Luke and Catherine just want what's best for

Cara. Hell, I get their concerns. I am an older version of the woman—living life only interested in the next chase I'll find myself in and always hoping I'll get the bad guy in the end. I wonder if I'll be able to simply walk away once I catch my ultimate conquest.

It seems so simple, but I'm not sure I'll be at peace after I catch the Marlin.

I take another sip of my martini and consider everything Luke said he would want for Cara. It's everything I can provide her, at least temporarily, for our arrangement.

The way Cara does not want to marry me should hurt my feelings, but it doesn't. We aren't exactly friends.

Fine.

We're the opposite of friends. Getting under her skin is one of my passions. Now, we have to be on the same team, and the thought of her becoming my wife is causing a strange feeling to stir inside. It goes beyond my pull to her. It feels almost primal.

Something about me wanting to be good for her, even under the circumstances, sounds... appealing. I want to be someone right for Cara.

I pull out my cell phone to text her to firm up our plans.

GRANT

Tomorrow. Courthouse at noon.

CARA

See you then, Sinclair.

I pocket my phone, not liking the way she's still using my last name.

"Sorry about that," Luke says as he returns.

"It's no problem. Tell me about how your partnerships are going."

"Right, where do I begin?"

I flag the server for another round of drinks as my old friend tells me about his business. It's a comfortable and safe discussion for us to have instead of me thinking about how I'm his daughter's type after all.

AFTER LEAVING the golf club with Luke, I decide to take a quick trip out to Charleston, South Carolina, for the afternoon. Well, quick isn't exactly true, but I'll be able to make it back in time to meet with Cara tomorrow afternoon. Flying private does have its perks.

The pull to do this somewhat right felt overwhelming as I drove home. That's when the idea hit me of what I need to do before we meet at the courthouse.

Even if this is a marriage of convenience, I need to make sure Cara has the best experience possible.

This is why I'm currently at my favorite jeweler in downtown Charleston, picking out an engagement ring and wedding band. In my packet from the agency was a simple gold band for me to wear. I'm assuming they gave her the same.

If Cara is going to be my wife in any capacity, then I'm not going to let her wear something simple like that. Not when it's my name on the marriage certificate with hers.

"What do you think, sir?" the jeweler, Pierre, asks.

I hold the three-and-a-half carat emerald-cut diamond ring in my hand and know it's perfect for Cara. It's something she would wear, not that I expect her to ever admit it.

"It's perfect."

"Excellent!"

"And the matching band?"

Pierre looks around his trays and finds the match to the engagement ring. It's in platinum, too, and a thin set of diamonds surrounds it.

"Is this it?" I ask.

"Yes, sir. We can always find something else for you to compare it to."

"No, this is wonderful. I'll take them both."

"Excellent news. I know you are assuming her ring finger size, but please come back, and we can adjust it at no cost to you if needed."

I am taking a gamble, but one part of my job is being able to size people up correctly—even when it comes to their ring sizes.

"Thank you. I appreciate that."

Pierre takes both rings and begins preparing their packaging.

Maybe it was a gamble taking it this far, but it feels like the right move.

Since I'm in Charleston, I'm going to visit with my friend Fisher, who moved here somewhat recently. He lives downtown with his fiancée, Ellie. Fisher agreed to meet me at a bar I own in the area—one of my many investments that a team runs in my absence.

The Blue Marlin Lounge is a go-to place in downtown Charleston and is named after the very elusive white whale of my own, the Marlin. A little homage to the villain of my story, whom I haven't been able to capture. Hopefully, that all ends with this next mission I'm about to embark on.

"Here you are, sir."

I look up to see that Pierre has the gifts wrapped and bagged already.

"Thank you," I say as I slide over my black credit card.

"My pleasure. I'll be right back," he says with the card

in his hand. He disappears once more, only this time to a nearby cash register.

As he returns with my card, I realize I may be in over my head when it comes to Cara. I've never had the urge to settle down, and I still don't, but the pull to make her happy is an overwhelming sensation.

It must be because of my relationship with her father. Luke would kill me if he knew I was marrying Cara. His finding out is a bridge we hopefully won't have to cross.

My plan is to marry Cara for the time being. I've secured all the necessary paperwork for us, so she won't need to worry about me taking her money or the companies she owns. Then, when all this is finished, we can get divorced. Clean and simple. No mess and nothing to worry about after the next few months.

"Here you are, sir. Thank you once again for your business."

"Thank you," I say.

"And if I may, I'm glad to see someone has finally captured your attention after all these years. She must be very special."

I study Pierre for just a moment. He has been my go-to for years.

"Thank you. She is."

Isn't that the damn truth?

She's the only one I've ever been tempted enough by, but also the one with whom this can never be real.

He gives me a warm smile as I take the bag and leave.

"DIDN'T THINK I'd find you in Charleston again anytime

soon," Fisher says as he slides into my private area at the Blue Marlin Lounge.

"Never thought you'd give up your life in Seattle for a woman," I taunt.

Fisher smirks and then orders a whiskey.

"What brings you here for such a short amount of time?" he asks.

"I had to pick something up. You know I favor Charleston over any of the businesses out in California."

"Which I'm sure are just as good."

"They are, but you know my pull to the area."

"That I do. Thinking of coming back for longer any time soon?"

The server distracts us both as she hands Fisher his cocktail. He takes a small drink before setting it down on the table.

"No. I have another trip that's going to take me away for longer than usual."

Fisher knows about my work, but we don't dare talk about it in detail in a busy public setting like this.

He gives me a curt nod before looking around the room. It's busy at this time of night.

"Where's Ellie?" I ask.

"She's out with her friend Harper."

"Harper?"

"She's one of the women who went out on the bachelorette party cruise a couple of years ago. The one you gave her VIP here for."

"Oh, right. She's with the boat captain?"

"That's right."

I lean forward to grab my cocktail, and Fisher does the same as we settle back in our seats.

"Are you in trouble?" he asks.

"I couldn't tell you if I was."

"Are you?"

I look around the room.

"No. Not yet."

"You know I'm here for you. If trouble happens, I'll be here."

"It might just come to that."

His jaw ticks, and I know Fisher is wishing I would have just gone to his house. I didn't because I knew my friend would want to know more than I can give him. We've always had a silent agreement in our friendship. I've helped him from time to time, and he's been a confidant for me.

It's rare to trust anyone once you've been in my line of work for a while. Most people will just let you down.

"You know you can trust me. And Ellie. And our friends here."

"I do."

I take a sip of my cocktail to buy some time.

"You'd like them. One day, I want you to come back here and take a real break."

I grin as I swirl what's left of my drink in front of me.

"Is it really a break if I've set up my retirement plan here?"

Fisher grins back.

"Now that's what I like to hear."

A server comes over, and I request another round plus a bottle of champagne.

"Champagne?" Fisher asks, slightly confused.

"Don't tell me Ellie and Harper won't be stopping by here on their way home."

"I think they'll be by any minute."

"Perfect. Then I'm afraid to say, I have to be going."

"Leaving me here?"

"Have to get back. Tomorrow, it all begins."

"What does?"

I stand and adjust my suit jacket.

"Forever, evidently."

The server stops by, and I take a drink of the fresh cocktail before setting it back on her tray. As I do, Ellie and her friend Harper come walking up.

"Hi, Grant," Ellie greets me.

"Looking as beautiful as ever, Ellie."

She goes in for a hug that I reciprocate. As I pull away, I put out my hand to say hello to her friend.

"And you must be Harper. Congratulations on your upcoming nuptials."

"Thank you. Not too much longer to go."

"Your fiancé is a lucky man."

"Thank you. You're as suave as Ellie said you would be," Harper teases.

"It's part of the job."

I look back to Ellie.

"Unfortunately, I have to run. Duty calls. But please, enjoy the evening here. I'll be back in Charleston soon enough."

"Oh, really?" Ellie says excitedly.

"I don't know what choice I have with your grumpy bastard."

Ellie and Harper laugh as they walk past me.

"It's good to see you," Ellie says.

"Take care of him."

"You know I will."

I look over at my friend Fisher, who's pretending to glare at me.

"Until next time," I say.

"Good luck," he answers.

Luck.

I'm always lucky.

I'd rather be lucky than good. At least I know luck has been on my side ever since Cara Collins came into the picture.

My lucky charm.

FIVE

Cara

"WHY ARE you picking out a *real* wedding ring for Grant? This isn't a *real* wedding, according to you," Ruby asks as she holds up the platinum wedding band. She continues to examine it in the light as she waits for my response.

I take it out of her grasp before handing it back over to the store clerk. I'm meeting Grant at the courthouse later today to get legally married. It's as real as can be, regardless of what Ruby or anyone else thinks.

The sanctity of marriage has always been important to me, which is why I've never actually been or wanted to get married.

For some reason, despite my better judgment, I trust that Grant truly believes this is the best route for us to take. I'm relying on this man whom I despise on the best day. I don't think he would mislead me like this.

There's something he isn't telling me about his past with

the Carolinas mafia, but I know, for the sake of finally catching the Kingpin, that I have to trust my partner.

I shiver at the thought of him, of all people, being my partner until death do us part.

"Who are you talking to in there?" Ruby asks.

I look over at my assistant and see an amused look. She often catches me in my head, playing out different scenarios.

"No one," I finally answer.

I roll my eyes and focus on the store clerk.

"I'll take this one, please."

"Of course. I'll be right back with the final total."

Ruby leans against the glass case filled with different men's wedding bands.

"Who would have guessed?" she asks.

"What?"

"I told you so."

I cross my arms over my chest, confused by what she's referencing.

"I told you that you were going to marry this man someday," she teases.

"Oh, fine. You did. I'll give you that. There's only one problem."

"What's that?"

"This isn't forever."

"The multi-thousand-dollar wedding band sure tells a different story."

Uncrossing my arms, I give her an annoyed look as I plant a hand on a jutted-out hip.

"I'm marrying him because it makes sense given our profession and the job we're about to go out on. Nothing more or less. It's a simple contract."

"A simple contract," she draws out.

"Yes. Plain and simple. As soon as the job is done, we'll get it annulled."

"Have you talked to him yet about this plan? Or how about the papers I had drawn up for you that you have refused to look at?"

The store clerk comes over, and I hand him a credit card without looking at the bill. I'm buying this ring regardless of its cost or anyone's opinion. I can't have my pretend husband wearing a ring that the agency gave him to wear.

"I don't care if it makes me look dumb; I'd rather not bring up the idea of a prenup."

"This marriage is just a contract; it isn't one for love. You need to protect yourself and your assets."

"Grant Sinclair may be a thorn in my side, but I trust him to do what's best for me. He wouldn't take all my assets or money."

Ruby's mouth tightens, and I know she's debating whether to say what's on her mind.

"Are you prepared for him to ask you for one?" she finally says.

"Here you go, Ms. Collins." The store clerk hands me back my credit card along with a slip of paper to sign. Once I pass it back to him, he hands over the wrapped ring box in a black gift bag.

"Thank you."

"My pleasure," he responds.

I take the bag and start to head out the front door, with Ruby following behind.

Putting my sunglasses on, we walk toward my car to head back to my house. It's time for me to get ready for my wedding.

"You haven't answered me," she says as we both get into my car.

"I don't know how I'll feel about it if he does. I'll do it if he wants me to."

"That simple?"

"Anything to keep this plain and simple, Ruby. It's just part of the job."

"Whatever you say, boss."

I rev the engine and pull onto the highway. I may be trying to come across as calm and collected about all of this, but she's right. There's a pit in my stomach that I know means I'll look at Grant differently if he asks me for one. I shouldn't feel this way, but I do.

The smart decision is to sign more contracts to protect our respective assets. I know that. I just can't help it that part of me wants to believe in something bigger than reality.

Deep down, because I only wanted to be married one time, there's just something unsettling about it all.

MY BAGS ARE PACKED and waiting in the trunk of the car. After the ceremony, Grant and I are heading to San Diego for a pretend honeymoon. It's a one-night stay at a nice hotel in case anyone goes digging into our situation.

Really, our plane leaves at 0600 hours tomorrow, so it's only practical that we both head out that way from Los Angeles.

When Grant's assistant, Rob, talked to Ruby about the idea, it made sense to me despite not wanting to be trapped in a hotel with the man overnight. If we're getting married and flying out of San Diego, it's practical to pretend like we're on a brief honeymoon before leaving for our new home in Charlotte.

It all makes sense, and that's part of the problem I have.

All this playing pretend feels real somehow. I have to keep reminding myself of why Grant and I are even doing this ahead of the mission. The truth of the matter is I keep getting confused because of the relationship that Grant and I have with one another.

All this time, I've thought of him as my rival, someone who gets on my last nerve and drives me to the brink of madness. In actuality, it feels almost right that this is who I'm marrying.

My mind needs to play catch-up with what's really happening here.

I'm a professional.

This is my job. None of it is real.

Yet... it's Grant. My dad's friend. The person who chases me around the world. The one who gets under my skin like no other and, in some way, has consistently been there for me.

As I conflate the two sides of Grant Sinclair, I have to come to terms with the fact that both of those versions of him are the man I'm marrying in ten minutes.

Standing before the courthouse, I know I have to put one foot in front of the other. My future husband is waiting behind those double doors for me to arrive and say, "I do."

I take a series of calming breaths and smooth out my short white lace dress. It has delicate sleeves, and the same lace pattern is against my chest area. It's a dress I would have picked out for myself for my actual wedding.

Even though my mother would want me to have an over-the-top wedding, if I were to marry anyone, it would still be like this. Something personal just between him and me.

I decided my high heels would be my *something blue*—pale blue with a hint of faux diamonds on the top near the toe area.

I walk up the steep steps with a bouquet in hand, knowing that I'm the soon-to-be Mrs. Sinclair, even if it's only on paper.

My long brown hair is straightened, and I look like I always imagined I would. Now, I wonder how seriously Grant will take this.

Is he behind those doors wearing a pair of cargo shorts and a fishing T-shirt?

I laugh as I step up the last step.

I would actually die of laughter if I ever saw Mr. Prim and Proper in anything other than a suit. Our days living together in marital bliss are going to be something else. What does a dressed-down Grant even look like?

I try to contain my amusement as I open the doors.

Stepping inside, I look around to find the courthouse entrance surprisingly packed. As I scan the room for Grant or Ruby, my eyes freeze on the man across the hall.

Grant is dressed in a tuxedo, one of the better ones I've seen him in. With his slightly graying, deep-black hair styled nicely, he looks like any bride's dream come true.

I have to keep reminding myself that this man is my fake husband.

My future husband wouldn't do the things that Grant has done to me. He wouldn't talk so brashly to me. He wouldn't tell me all the lies I've been told.

Then I smirk.

Okay, maybe he would talk dirty to me, but I'd like to keep that kind of banter for my future husband.

As I slowly continue forward, Grant does the same until we've both walked the remaining distance, meeting in the middle.

Maybe a positive sign of what could be.

"Cara."

"It's Cara today?" I ask with a cock of my eyebrow.

"Can't be my lucky charm. That's for the field."

"Then just Cara works."

"There's nothing *just* about you today, Cara."

Grant's eyes scan the length of my body, starting from my heels, then up my long legs until finally, his gaze is back on my eyes.

"You look beautiful," he rasps.

"Thank you," I whisper.

My throat feels constricted as heat crawls up my cheeks.

"You look handsome."

Grant grins widely.

"What?" I ask.

"So there is a first time for everything."

My eyebrows furrow together as I try to understand what jab he's making.

"What?" I ask again.

"A compliment from Cara Collins. Never thought I'd see the day."

"Oh, stop," I say with a roll of my eyes.

I bite down on my lower lip to try and contain my smile. Without giving anything away, I search the room for Ruby and see her inside a glass office with someone who has to be the judge and Grant's assistant.

"Is that where we'll be?" I ask, looking back up at him.

Grant's eyes have been focused on me this entire time, and I feel a prick of unease from the sensation. I don't like being anyone's primary focus. Maybe that's from the job, but it's always a bad sign of what's to come.

"It is," he murmurs.

"Good. Should we get going?"

"After you," he says with his arm extended.

I clear my throat and give him a small nod before starting to walk in that direction. With my shoulders pulled back and stomach tightened, I try to reclaim any part of my usual confidence that I have in this role.

Keeping the façade of who I am in work mode around Grant is going to be crucial if I'm going to make it through these unusual circumstances.

I go to pull the door open when his broad frame overshadows it. His hand covers mine on the handle, stopping me.

"There are some things you and I should talk about alone."

I look up over my shoulder and wait.

"Cara," he murmurs.

I turn and face him fully.

"What is it?"

"I know this isn't what you've probably imagined yourself having to do."

"It's not," I answer playfully.

Grant's expression gets more stoic.

"It's okay. It's part of our jobs. I'm a big girl, remember?"

"I know, but I have to get this off my chest."

"Okay."

Grant looks more serious than I've ever seen him before. I give him my undivided attention, wanting him to know I take this seriously too.

"I promise to take care of you during this mission. While you're my wife on paper, you're mine to protect. I promise to not let you get hurt in any capacity. I will take care of you in sickness and in health. You and I both know we're bound to run into a few issues requiring care. Do you understand?"

I suck in a deep breath as his words penetrate.

"Yes," I whisper.

"Good. I know we won't make personal vows in there, so I wanted to make sure you knew where I'm at before we move forward."

Grant goes to open the door, only this time it's me stopping him. He peers down at me, and for the first time in my life, I feel small. Normally, my five-foot-ten stature makes me feel bigger than even some men, only not around Grant.

"I promise to take care of *you*, Grant Sinclair. While you're my husband, nothing will happen to you either. Do you understand?"

Grant's eyes simmer with something different than they ever have around me. I'm not sure what it is. Certainly not desire or lust, but something deeper than that.

"I do."

"Good."

I smile widely.

"Now let's go get married. What do you say?"

He grins back.

"After you, Ms. Collins."

I pull open the door but turn back slightly before going into the room.

"Not for much longer."

Grant makes a slight groan that I must be imagining in this moment. I focus back on the people waiting and mentally prepare to say I do.

"You're so pretty!" Ruby squeals.

Although she knows what this situation really is, Ruby

is a sucker for love. Of course she's excited to be here as my witness.

"Thank you," I answer.

"Ms. Collins, I'm Rob, Mr. Sinclair's assistant. It's a pleasure to meet you," he says as we shake hands.

"You as well."

I focus on the judge behind his desk.

"Ms. Collins, Mr. Sinclair. Let's get you two married."

He steps out in front of his desk. Grant and I position ourselves in front of him as Ruby and Rob take seats in nearby office chairs.

"Thank you for doing this for us, Sam," Grant says.

"A favor paid back," Sam replies.

Grant focuses his attention on me.

Sam starts to run through the motions of the wedding. Grant and I repeat our lines to one another. It's all very impersonal.

I think I'll take the impromptu vows we made to one another outside of this room as our real vows instead.

As I stare at my soon-to-be husband, I realize that this could be a good situation for the two of us. Despite my concerns with some of the ways he's let me down in the field, I don't think Grant will let me down as a husband.

Maybe Grant doesn't have to be my rival; maybe he can become a friend when this whole scenario is over with.

It's time for us to exchange rings.

Ruby gets up and hands me Grant's first. Holding the platinum band in my hand, I play with it slightly for a moment. As I hold his hand in mine and slip the ring on his finger, suddenly, this impersonal situation feels like the most personal thing I've ever experienced.

Grant's hand flexes as he takes it back. Rob stands and hands Grant my ring. I notice that he also purchased a new ring instead of using the one that the agency had given us.

It feels as though Grant and I have been on the same page about everything since we found out about this mission and the need to work together. Almost as if we've been having the same line of thought on how to move forward, just like partners would.

This may all be pretend, but there's something more happening between us as we exchange rings. It's not love or lust but rather an understanding and appreciation of the situation we're in.

It feels as though Grant and I both have mutual respect for one another.

This shouldn't have been this unexpected, but given how much turmoil and animosity we face in the field, I just didn't see it coming. I had been so busy worrying about the façade that I didn't consider the truth that could be between us.

It's all a promising sign that perhaps over the next few months, we'll be able to make it out alive, or at least not kill each other.

"I now pronounce you man and wife. You may kiss your bride," Sam says and takes a large step back.

Grant takes my hands in his and gently plays with my new piece of jewelry. He focuses on our connection just for a moment before gazing into my eyes.

He steps forward, and I notice that same look from earlier has returned to his face. It's powerful and means more to me than he probably realizes.

As he goes in to kiss me, my heartbeat quickens. Before he places his lips on mine, he pauses.

"Are you okay with this?"

"Yes," I whisper.

Grant gives me a slight gesture before our lips connect. Fireworks ignite in my body as our connection holds. It's as if sparks are going off everywhere from this slight touch, and I can't get enough.

The way his smooth lips feel against mine is undeniable. If it were anyone else I was experiencing this next-level kiss with, I would naturally want to deepen it.

I pull back, needing to get away from the all-consuming feeling of wanting more and watch as a startled look flickers over Grant's expression.

This time, as I stare into his eyes, there's no confusion as to what I'm seeing. Grant looks exactly the way I must look to him, utterly taken aback by what just transpired between us.

Ruby and Rob clap beside us, bringing us out of our lust-filled haze.

"Now, time for the paperwork," Sam says as he walks behind his desk. Grant and I take the two seats in front of it as Ruby and Rob stand nearby.

I feel as though the fireworks are still shooting off underneath my skin just from being in his proximity after that kiss.

"Here is the marriage license. If you can sign here, and Mrs. Sinclair, if you can please sign here," Sam says nonchalantly.

It's the first time that I'm being referred to as Mrs. Sinclair. The idea of it suddenly doesn't seem as far-fetched as it did minutes ago.

"And then, if you two can please sign here and here," Sam says to Ruby and Rob.

"Are you okay?" Grant whispers to me.

"Yes," I murmur.

"Good."

Sam places the certificate in front of Grant before trying to find another set of paperwork.

"And here is the prenuptial agreement. I take it all attorneys have seen it?" Sam asks.

My eyes nearly bug out of my head as I focus on Grant.

"You want a prenup?" I croak.

Grant studies me for just a moment before looking at Sam.

"This will no longer be necessary," he says as he stands.

I stand up as well, still in confusion. That's a sudden change of pace.

"It's okay if you do. My team recommended it as well," I add.

I need to play the role of Cara Collins, private contractor extraordinaire, not Cara Collins, lovesick bride. If Grant wants this, I will sign it with no ill will.

Grant cups my shoulders in his hands, and the warmth sets off sparks all over again. He rubs his hands gently on them.

"I understand."

Two simple words that hold so much meaning.

In a haze, I gesture my gratitude.

How can he simply understand? There's more to unpack at a future date.

"If that's all, then enjoy your evening. I have a case I need to get to," Sam says.

I try to put my professional mask back on and not dive into the feelings I'm experiencing as I follow Grant out of the office. Ruby and Rob are right behind us. I can't show any hint of confusion in front of anyone after that interaction.

"Cara, I'll take us to San Diego."

"I have a car service waiting outside."

"I'm sure Ruby here can take care of that," he counters.

Grant's eyes stay focused on me. He's not letting me out of his sight. Why does it make heat crawl up my skin and a hint of pink flush my cheeks?

"Okay."

I turn to Ruby, whose eyes are twinkling.

"Let's go get my bags."

"Perfect," Grant answers.

Another time I'm simply going along with Grant Sinclair's plans. I hope this doesn't become a pattern.

SIX

Grant

THE DRIVE from Los Angeles to San Diego is a relatively easy one. It's usually a time when I appreciate the ability to think while driving along the coastline. Not this trip; instead, I find myself sitting next to the version of Cara Collins that I periodically see out in the field.

She's determined, fierce, and confident. It's as if saying "I do" sealed our fate for how this was going to go. A business transaction and nothing more. Not that I'm complaining, because it is business.

The version of Cara that I saw at the courthouse was entirely different. She was vulnerable, and I knew that this wedding was something that held meaning to her that she would never admit to me.

I realized that as soon as I saw her step inside the courthouse, and then time and time again. All I wanted to do was tell her how she made me feel right then.

I did my best to show her how this would go without crossing any lines.

As I glance over at the wind blowing in her hair, she looks like a model from any of the high-fashion magazines, not a spy ready to take on the mafia.

A sting of guilt twists inside me.

I've seen Cara out there in action, but it's entirely different now that she's my wife. What if something were to happen to her? I meant every word I said before we got married. I would protect her with my life in any situation.

Maybe I didn't think this through because I'm experiencing a new weight of wanting to make sure she's taken care of.

"Are you okay over there?" Cara asks.

I glance over to see her leaning against the passenger side doorframe, letting the scarf covering her hair float out the window with the wind.

"Fine."

Looking back at the road, I pick up the speed; anything to get out of this car and have some time alone to think. I should have just had her meet me there, but even I need to remember that part of this ruse is following the steps I would take with any other contractor in our line of work.

"Fine?" she muses.

"Yes, it's a word."

"If you say so."

I twist my hands around the steering wheel tightly. She's trying to get under my skin now, but I have to play into this hand.

"And what's wrong with that?" I ask.

"Please, don't play dumb now. No one has ever said the word *fine* and meant it."

"Maybe I am."

"Maybe you're more bland and typical than I imagined."

I smirk as I change lanes.

"Maybe I am," I taunt.

Cara pops off her sunglasses and soaks me in. Pretending like I'm not suddenly interested in her attention is harder than I imagined it would be. More truths are coming to light.

"I don't get you, Sinclair."

"Not much to get."

"Really?" she asks, drawing it out.

"Really."

"Then tell me about you."

"Cara Collins is finally trying to get to know me. Never thought the day would come."

"We have another two hours. Have to pass the time somehow."

"That's it? Passing the time by getting to know your new husband."

She sighs and turns to face forward with her glasses still off.

I'm not sure why, but the sudden distance she just put between us by shutting down is another feeling I'm not a fan of. Lately, there seem to be a lot of new ways that Cara is able to affect me.

She tilts her head back on the seat and closes her eyes. The way the sun illuminates her skin makes her look like someone I want to actually talk to. Another new feeling I'll have to dive into eventually.

"I'm from Charleston."

I hear the way the leather seat crinkles as she goes back to her original position with a better ability to look my way.

"Really?"

"Yes, really. My parents moved to Charleston from Ireland before I was born."

She shifts beside me.

"I didn't know that."

"Without going into all my gritty details, I ended up in California working for a security agency, and one thing led to the next. Now I'm running my company."

"Why do you still go out in the field?"

I give her a light laugh.

I wonder the same thing every day.

"No, what I meant is, your operation is much larger than mine. And I know you own about a dozen other businesses..."

"Well, they aren't all—" I start.

She holds up a hand to cut me off.

"Or investments. Whatever you want to call them. Point is, you don't need to be the one out and about in the field. Frankly, you don't need jobs from the agency either."

Not a question. My little lucky charm has done her research.

"I like being out in the field. While I still can. Plus, the agency gives me access that sometimes is difficult to get without working for the government."

"While you still can?"

"I'm not getting any younger. Once we catch the Marlin, I'll probably rein in my activity."

Cara laughs loudly, only instead of grating on me, it sounds like the sweetest melody. Another situation I'll think about later.

"Sinclair," she says through stifled laughter.

"Am I amusing you?"

"Grant. Come on. You told me you're forty-nine years old. That's young. I mean, my dad is old, but you aren't."

A sting courses through me. She's comparing me to her goddamn dad.

"Maybe I feel like I am."

"Back to this?"

"Just saying, Collins, time goes by quickly. I may be almost fifty years old, but my body, and frankly, my mind, feel like I've been through enough to last me a lifetime."

A few minutes of silence pass.

"You know I don't think you're anything like my dad, right?" she asks.

It comes out more serious than our playfulness has been the entire car ride.

"Don't worry, I know you don't. I also know a girl like you shouldn't end up with a fifty-year-old man like me."

"Why is that?"

"Don't worry about it."

She hums.

"Whatever you say, Sinclair."

Cara crosses her arms over her chest and brings one of her legs up to fold under her body on the seat. She's closing herself off to me again.

Good.

Cara opening up to me will do neither of us any good in this line of work.

THE SUITE at the Draper Hotel is meant for a couple on their honeymoon. In mostly white and gold designs, it'd be the perfect place if I were trying to impress my new bride.

This is my assistant Rob's doing. He asked what I wanted, and I told him we needed a suite for space, but this is beyond that. Hell, we could have gotten any number of other rooms at this hotel instead of this one that would have worked.

The Draper Hotel is my favorite place to stay in San Diego, all because of the beachfront view. The very one I'm staring out at right now, and Cara is too.

"It's beautiful," she says.

"It is," I say from behind where she stands.

Maybe I am talking about the woman in front of me too.

"Think we could go down there at sunset?"

"It's a must."

Cara laughs softly, and I watch as her body vibrates.

"What?"

"I get it."

"What's that?"

"The charm of the great Grant Sinclair. If this is the type of date you normally provide to your flock of women, then I get why you're so infamous."

Another unintentional sting.

"Don't believe every rumor you hear."

I leave the best view I've had in ages and head to the nearby in-room bar. Closing the short distance, I pull out a tiny whiskey bottle from the mini fridge and pour it into a glass.

"Is there another one of those in there?" Cara calls out.

"There is."

I pull out the second mini bottle of whiskey and pour Cara's into the other glass available.

I hear the sound of her heels against the tile as she approaches.

"I don't think you're sleeping with women in every city," she says.

"Just LA?" I quip.

"Maybe LA and New York," she teases.

My shoulders relax, and I had no idea they were as tense as they were. We're not even on the mission yet, and I have a feeling neither of us is acting like ourselves.

"I'm going to go in the other room and take a shower. Maybe change out of this wedding dress. Then I'll take that drink," she muses.

As she walks away, I feel a sense of loneliness.

"Collins?" I shout as I turn toward the doorway.

She stills and looks over her shoulder at me.

"You looked beautiful today. It's a pity we didn't take any pictures."

Cara bites down on her plump lower lip, and it stirs something inside me.

"Come in here," she says while gesturing for me to follow.

I do immediately.

She sits down on the bed and pulls out her cell phone from the purse she was carrying.

"Sit down next to me," she demands.

And I do immediately once again.

Tossing the purse onto the bed, she then opens the camera on her cell phone. She makes it so the camera's focus is on us, sitting together.

I put my arm around the back of her waist. Cara's breath hitches from the contact before she pulls it together.

"Smile," she says.

We both face the camera, and she takes a few shots of us together.

Lowering the phone in her hand, Cara turns to me and smiles. It's breathtaking to witness.

"Now we do." She beams.

I clear my throat and adjust the tie around my neck.

"I'll be out on the balcony with our drinks," I offer.

Cara nods, and I see a hint of something in her eyes that I'm imagining is desire. It can't be because all of this is just pretend.

"See you out there," I rasp.

She smirks before disappearing into the bathroom.

OUT ON THE BALCONY, the whiskeys are sweating as I wait for Cara to get out of the shower.

The sound of waves crashing in the distance makes me realize that this is going to be a rare moment of calmness before the metaphorical storm.

Fuck. Not metaphorical at all, really.

I may die in the next few months. A thought I have come to terms with.

It's not that I'm terrible at my job or anything of the like; this is one of the most dangerous roles I'll play, and I'll be doing it with Cara by my side. This isn't exactly the setting I imagined when I would finally have a chance to catch the Marlin.

My phone buzzes in my jacket pocket. Pulling it out, I see it's my assistant, Rob.

"This is Grant."

"Mr. Sinclair. How is the Draper?"

"You got us one of the best rooms in the hotel."

"Fantastic news. I wasn't sure if my connection would be able to get one on short notice."

I sigh as I rub my eyebrows.

"Rob. It's a little much. She's not my actual wife, and this isn't my honeymoon."

"You didn't see the way she looked at you?"

I settle back in the deck chair.

"No. She wasn't looking at me any which way."

"Then what was the deal about the prenup paperwork? Anyone would assume they would have been drawn."

"She trusts me because of our personal connection outside of work."

"Right. That's why she didn't sign."

"It's neither here nor there. It's done, and this room is too romantic. Keep that in mind for next time."

"Whatever you say, boss."

"Good."

I lean forward and place my elbows on my knees as one arm hangs in front of me.

"Anything else to report?" I ask.

"No, sir. Well..."

"What is it?"

"I know this marriage is all a sham, but one question, if you don't mind."

"I never mind; you know that."

"Why didn't you have her sign the papers? You're normally too cautious for your own good."

My eyes widen slightly at the question. I did walk right into that one.

"I have no goddamn idea."

Rob chuckles.

"Have a good night, sir."

"Night."

I toss my phone onto the table with our drinks and get up to remove my suit jacket and tie. After discarding them, I undo a couple of top buttons on my dress shirt and roll up my sleeves.

"Still as beautiful as it was earlier," Cara murmurs.

My line of sight veers toward where she stands, and my breath is taken away. I see Cara in the most dressed-down version of her I could imagine. A black sweater with black jeans and a pair of wedged black tennis shoes.

"Take a seat."

"If you insist," she says with a small laugh.

Cara sits down next to me and picks up her drink. She waits for me to follow as she holds it in the air.

Taking mine, I mimic her pose.

"To us," she says.

"To us, Mrs. Sinclair," I say with a smirk.

Taking a sip, I let the brown liquid burn as it goes down my throat. Cara eyes me suspiciously as she takes a sip of hers.

"Ready for tomorrow?" she asks.

"You know how it goes."

"I do."

Cara looks out to the ocean.

"Something wrong?"

"No, of course not."

I study her expression as she tries not to look in my direction.

"If we're going to be partners, then you have to tell me what you're thinking."

She glances over, and I see a hint of a smile playing on her lips.

"What's with the nickname of lucky charm?"

"You should be ever so grateful for all of them," I taunt.

"Come on, Grant. Really? Pick which one you want to use. It's lucky charm, darling, and I'm sure there are others."

"Never, Collins."

I shoot her a flirty wink.

"Oh, please. Play it your way."

She gets comfortable and kicks her feet up underneath

where she's sitting. The platform sneakers are off the side of the chair as she leans onto one of the armrests.

"Do you still want to go down and watch the sunset?"

Cara looks over at me and gives me a small shrug.

"You're not a shrugger. Don't go playing damsel in distress with me now."

Cara laughs freely as she shrugs again.

"This is nice," I say, causing her to tense momentarily before relaxing again.

"It is. Almost as if we really will be able to handle this whole partnership."

"I have no doubt we'll be able to."

"Are you sure?" she whispers.

"Yes. I promise. We've got this covered."

"I hope so. I'd like to have the Kingpin down, once and for all."

"It has been a while since you've been chasing the Kingpin."

"Not that long," she retorts.

"You're right; however, I'd like to put this whole mess behind us as soon as possible."

A comfortable silence lingers between us on the patio as we stare out to the ocean, watching the sun begin to set.

I get up and grab two more mini bottles of whiskey and pour them into each of our glasses.

Cara murmurs her thanks as I sit down, and it's back to us being relaxed in each other's presence.

"Will you tell me how you're connected to this ring?" Cara asks after some time.

"Yes."

"Not tonight. I think I may call it an early night soon. I don't think I can handle going down to watch the sunset."

"Another time. I promise."

"Don't go making promises you can't keep."

"With you, I just don't want to lie."

Cara yawns and starts to stretch. It's still relatively early, but it has been an eventful few days.

"I'll take the couch. Okay if I grab a quick shower?"

"Yes, of course. Be my guest."

I leave Cara outside and head back into the room. Pulling out my grooming kit, I head into the bathroom.

Staring at myself in the mirror, I look as exhausted as I feel. I won't let anyone know, but I'm damn tired of all this running around. Maybe after I catch the Marlin, I'll feel reinvigorated, or it'll be the final sign that I'm meant to become a normal businessman.

I take a quick shower so that Cara is able to get to bed soon. Even with this large of a suite, it only came with one king-size bed. The double room suites must have all been taken.

It's fine; I've slept on rocks before on a mission, so a pull-out sofa will be good.

As I get out, I quickly dry off and realize that I must have left my pajama pants out in the living room area. I wrap the towel around my waist and walk out of the room to fetch them.

"What the hell!" Cara shrieks.

"What?" I ask, stunned.

Cara's eyes rake over my body, and I follow her line of sight and grin.

I suppose my torso is still naked.

I can't help but enjoy the way she's drinking in every inch of me. I work damn hard for this body, and for once, someone I want to appreciate the way I look currently does.

"Like what you see?" I taunt.

Cara's eyes snap up to mine, and a flame of desire quickly turns to frustration.

"We don't have that kind of marriage. Get dressed."

She tosses me my clothes, and I catch them against my chest.

"Whatever you say, Collins."

Well, this is an interesting turn of events. I just caught Cara checking me out, and I definitely liked it.

SEVEN

Cara

GRANT SINCLAIR HAS no right to do what he has been doing to me.

The man has gotten inside my head, and even worse, he's made me trust him. *Him*, of all the people I trust. I can probably count the number of people I trust on two hands. Now Grant has weaseled his way onto that list.

And now, he's gone and made me have to admit to myself that I'm very attracted to how he looks.

The way the beads of water rolled down his chiseled chest as he glanced around the living room for his pajamas was absolutely infuriating. During that moment, his arms naturally flexed as he held on tightly to that towel, and it was outright uncalled-for behavior.

The worst part of it all? I had to go and see the outline of his twitching cock against the towel when I knew he wasn't even hard!

We moved in silence around each other as he got

dressed in the bedroom and then made his way out to the living room again to set up his bed on the sofa. Meanwhile, I went into the bedroom and got under the covers as soon as I could.

I feel so unlike myself around him these days, and it bothers me. Ever since this situation started to pull back the curtain of who I am during my day-to-day, he's been getting more chances to see the real me. It's as if the walls around us are crumbling down, and it's been only a few days.

There's no way I can continue to be this version of myself around Grant. Tomorrow morning will be here before we know it. I need a good night's sleep in order to be ready to work tomorrow.

I tighten the covers around my neck and shut my eyes.

Trying to get sleep seems almost impossible, knowing that Grant is mere feet away from me.

The sound of the sofa squeaking distracts me, and I know he must be twisting and turning on it. I don't care how fancy of a hotel we're at, no one wants to sleep on a pull-out sofa if you don't have to.

Only in this case, he can't help it. Sure, I'm glad he was a gentleman and offered me the bed, but I wouldn't possibly get any sleep if he were in here. My body feels like a million needles are pricking into it because of Grant's presence as it is. I can't even think about how I would feel with him inches away.

I fluff my pillow underneath and try to focus on letting sleep take over. I rarely have these kinds of issues falling asleep. Like I'm sure Grant is, too, I'm used to getting some shut-eye in the most uncomfortable situations.

Minutes pass by, but they feel like hours. The silence in my room is deafening. It's the total opposite of the way the comfortable silence took over between us on the balcony.

"Fuck," I mutter.

I have a feeling I'll be muttering those words a lot when it comes to being around Grant.

Sitting up in bed, the sheets fall down around my waist as I run a hand through my hair. I check out my pajamas to make sure they are acceptable for a platonic friend to see me in.

"Sinclair!" I shout.

"What is it, Collins? Some of us need sleep."

I roll my eyes as I lean back on one hand against the bed.

"If I have to hear you tossing and turning out there, neither of us will be getting quality sleep for tomorrow. You can come in here. Just stay on your side."

I hear Grant getting out of the pull-out bed and padding across the floor to the bedroom. Within seconds, he's leaning against my bedroom doorframe, looking like he's mine. His bare chest is just as I remembered it, and his low-slung pajama pants tease his defined abdomen.

"Don't you own a shirt?" I groan.

Grant smiles widely.

"Glad to know you think I'm so pretty, but no funny business, Collins. I need my beauty sleep," he teases as he crosses the room to the other side of the bed.

"Please. I'm the one who needs sleep. Stay on your half of the bed."

Grant lifts the covers and slips onto the bed. I face the opposite direction and try not to look around. It doesn't prevent me from feeling his presence.

"Thanks, Collins."

"No problem, Sinclair."

A deep rumble sounds in the room, and I can't help but smile.

"Hey, Grant?"

"Yeah?"

"Wipe that smug smile off your face."

He laughs before he twists onto his side.

NATURALLY, I woke up at three in the morning after going to sleep too early last night. It was for the best. I was able to shower and dress, all while Grant stayed asleep in the bed we shared last night.

Packing my small bag was easy enough as well. Now I debate whether to wake up my new husband, as we are inching closer to when we need to be at the airport.

It doesn't matter how frequently I take private planes, a part of me will always want to get there as early as possible, as if it were a commercial flight.

This is something I've learned to tone down over the years, but if anything, I'm going to let myself be who I am... even if that means arriving at a private airport earlier than I should.

Heading into the bedroom, I walk over to Grant's side of the bed. His arms are flexed behind his head, and all I can see are the muscles I've recently discovered I enjoy staring at, taunting me.

I've never really taken a good look at Grant before this. Of course I've looked at him, but there's something different about watching him in this state. He sleeps peacefully, far better than I usually can.

I probably woke up a dozen times last night, tossing and turning while my mind raced alongside the nerves in my body.

"Sinclair."

No response.

"*Grant.*"

Still nothing.

I rest my hands on my hips and hang my head back in frustration.

"This man," I whisper.

"My wonderful husband is what I think you meant to say," Grant rasps.

His husky tone is unexpected and sends a jolt of electricity through my body. I want to take a step back but can't. If I did, then he would catch on quickly about the way he makes me feel these days.

"We leave in ten. Get ready."

I walk away and leave Grant in the room to get dressed.

In the living room part of the suite, I pour myself a cup of the coffee I had delivered earlier and add sugar to it.

Sitting down in the single chair next to my bags, I wait for Grant. As I take a drink of the hot coffee, I hear his shower turning off and then some fumbling closer to the door.

I take a few steadying, deep breaths. They help me compose myself during times of distress.

Good. He's almost ready. We can get out of here, finally —move onto the mission at hand and have less one-on-one time where we try to get to know each other.

I need to get a handle on these newfound feelings.

I wince.

I do not have feelings for Grant Sinclair.

Abruptly, I stand upright and fix my blazer, then grab my suitcase, duffle bag, tote bag, and purse.

"Heading out. See you on the plane," I shout.

Without giving him a chance to answer, I walk out the hotel door.

I may not have feelings for Grant, and this may be a mission, but I need some space to breathe without him in my proximity after the past twenty-four hours.

I rush out the exit and step into the waiting car service. When I close the car door, I let the driver know someone needs to pick up Grant too. He calls it in and says someone will also notify Mr. Sinclair.

Good.

That's handled.

"I DIDN'T TAKE you as a runner, Collins."

I perk up at the sound of Grant's deep voice as he steps onto the plane.

"I had some work I had to do. It's not my fault you sleep in ahead of a mission."

Grant grins as he plops his bag down on the side of his chair and takes the open seat in front of me.

His eyebrows shoot up, almost testing if I'll say anything else.

"I'm never late," I continue.

"Believe me, I already knew that about you."

"Let's not pretend as if you know me after a short time together."

"Maybe not."

I roll my eyes as the flight attendant appears.

Grant and all his *maybe-nots* are going to drive me crazy if he continues.

"Good morning. Can I get you anything to drink?" she asks Grant.

"Yes, please. A double espresso."

"Coming right up. And anything else for you, Mrs. Sinclair?"

I flinch at the name.

Regrouping immediately, I pull on my jacket and give her a small no.

"Please let me know if you need another latte or anything else at any time," she says before walking away.

"Don't forget, you're already my wife here," Grant whispers.

My head darts over to see his smug expression.

"Don't you forget, I could kill you with my bare hands."

I flash him my widest smile, and he laughs.

"My kind of foreplay."

Grant looks around the seats and finds a neatly folded paper on top of a nearby table.

"Reading the newspaper still?"

"It's important to see what's being shared with the masses."

Grant pulls out a pair of black glasses from his jacket pocket and sets them, along with the newspaper, on the table in front of us.

He takes off his jacket and neatly folds it over the chair next to him.

I try to focus on the device that I'm holding. Right now, I'm definitely interested in these blueprints and not the way Grant looks in a button-up.

"Reading anything interesting?" he asks.

I look up to see he's sitting back down, and our flight attendant is bringing him his requested espresso.

"Just looking over the homes in the neighborhood."

"Let's pull it up on the big screen and go over it together."

I sigh as I set it down in my lap.

"I think you can manage going over it separately."

"I could, but that wouldn't make either of us very good partners, now would it?"

"Fine. I'll put it up until takeoff. Which we can now do since you've arrived."

Grant smirks as he downs the entire drink and sets the small cup on the table.

"Would have been here with you if you had waited all of five minutes."

I cross one leg over the other and let my shoulders relax.

"Let's get one thing straight here. I may be your wife, but I'm not your mother or your babysitter, so get up earlier if you don't want to miss our travel times."

"Believe me, I don't need any of the three."

A slight sting since I am technically his wife.

I give him a pointed stare that he returns. It's a battle to see who will break eye contact first. Why do I get the feeling this is going to keep happening in the future?

"If you can please fasten your seat belts, we'll be taking off shortly," the flight attendant says.

"Thank you," I answer.

Looking around my waist, I buckle up, and I swear I hear the hint of a victory cheer coming from Grant. I peer up at him as I fasten my seat belt to see another smug expression.

"It would have been rude for us not to acknowledge her," I say.

"I don't disagree."

"We can review all the original plans I had in the air and some of the foundational materials that will still be relevant."

"Sounds good."

"Then I think once we settle into our home sweet home,

we can scout out the area and acclimate. Then revise our plans?"

"Solid idea."

I study him. Something is off with the way he's being so agreeable.

"What is it?"

"Before we go on our stroll around the neighborhood, I think you'll have to learn what I know."

"And what's that?"

"Who Ace is to the Carolinas mafia."

I lean back and grasp the ends of the armrests tightly.

"Deal."

Grant's eyebrows shoot up in surprise.

"You're not the only one who can be agreeable," I tease.

I can't help but laugh.

"What is it?" he asks.

"The past forty-eight hours or so have been the most agreeable time of my life. I can't wait for it to be over."

"Don't go wishing away what hasn't happened yet. I'm glad I could domesticate such a wild cat."

"Please," I sneer.

Grant beams that he got under my skin once more. At least we're back to the old way of talking to each other.

The flight attendant reviews the safety plans and then takes her seat at the front of the aircraft as the pilot shares that we're next in line for takeoff.

"Before I forget..."

Grant starts to pull a bag out of his briefcase and carefully sets it in front of me.

"What is it?"

"Open it."

"I don't do gifts."

"Maybe you'll do this one."

"Grant..." I trail off.

"Just open it. I promise it's for the job."

I sigh and lean forward to get the bag. Placing it on top of my device, I pull out a black velvet box.

Instantly, I gasp, and my hand shoots over my mouth.

My eyebrows furrow together as I discard the bag, and both hands rest on it. Trying not to let Grant see that I'm shaking, I slowly open it to find the most gorgeous engagement ring I have ever seen.

More importantly, it's perfect for me.

"The agency didn't give this to you."

"No. No, they didn't."

My heart flutters from the gesture.

"Why? Why did you do this?"

"You're my wife. You needed a proper engagement ring."

Finally getting the courage, I meet his eyes.

"We both already upgraded the wedding bands for each other. Which, by the way, thank you. But this? This is too much. I can't accept it."

Grant's eyes darken as his jaw twitches.

"You can, and you will."

"Tell me the truth then. Why did you do this?"

"Like I said, you're my wife. I wanted this to be special for you, regardless of whether it's a sham of a marriage."

I bob my head up and down as I think. We're taking off into the air as I try to find the right words to convey how special it actually is to me.

"Thank you."

"You don't have to thank me. If this were real, you would have gotten it the night I met you in the field."

I chuckle.

"Then why didn't I get it? Or does Ace not give his lucky charm engagement rings?" I tease.

He finally looks relaxed once again.

"Another time, we'll have to talk about our pasts together."

I agree. I've almost forgotten everything that is Grant Sinclair. All the back and forth, the betrayal, the desire he instills in me during our chase.

"Another time."

EIGHT

Grant

THE NEIGHBORHOOD we're living in is exactly how I assumed it would be. It's filled with nothing but manicured lawns, and oak trees line the streets. It's charming at best.

Little would anyone know that these homes are occupied by the people responsible for most of the crime in the city and throughout North and South Carolina.

Being here is like being transported into a past life of mine. One that neither Dodger nor Cara really knows about yet.

As part of our jobs, at any given time, you have to play the part. It's not all about showing up, catching the bad guy, and saving the day. Sometimes, it requires more finesse than that to find out the information you or your employer wants to know.

This is why I have no choice but to break the news to Cara that our next-door neighbor is a friend of mine in the Carolinas mafia, Brad the Bull.

Maybe I won't have to tell her how Brad got the nickname. Although, knowing Cara, I will.

"What do you think, darling?" I ask.

Cara's been walking in and out of each room of our temporary home together, inspecting every detail. She's back in work mode after that plane ride. There is no sign of how she feels about being here or what she thinks of the house.

Dodger asked me to confirm where Brad lived, and that was the basis of picking this home.

"It'll do," she says as she approaches the kitchen island.

"Good."

"Okay, so now that we have a feel for the neighborhood and discussed some of the plans, why don't you finally tell me what you've been keeping from me?"

I swallow thickly.

"What do you mean?"

"Come on, Sinclair."

Does she already know more than what I've shared?

Her eyes widen as her nails tap on the island.

"You told me you'd share who Ace is to these people. There's nothing about that in these files. I need you to tell me all the details."

"Right," I say, relieved. "Living room?"

"Okay," she says with a slight shrug.

I let Cara lead the way into the all-white living room. The chairs are white, the throw blankets are white, and even the throw pillows on top of the sectional sofa are white. It's just frankly clean-looking and doesn't feel homelike at all.

"I know this is pretend, but maybe we can redecorate here. It could even be a bonding activity for you and one of the wives."

Cara looks around the room, perplexed as to what I'm referring to.

"It's a blank canvas... literally. It's so alarming."

"Or it's refreshing?" she offers.

"Keep the idea in your back pocket at least."

"Right," she says, confused.

I hold onto my knees as I sit across from her on the other end of the sofa.

"Let's hear it," she says.

"Our next-door neighbor is going to be our way into the Kingpin's underground deals. His name is Brad Covington. I know him as Brad the Bull."

Cara gets serious as she waits for me to continue.

"Maybe five or six years ago, I was hired by someone anonymously."

"It's common enough."

"He hired me to get information on his client who had gone rogue. That's when I found myself meeting Brad for the first time. It wasn't here in Charlotte but in a smaller town, maybe fifty miles north of here."

Cara nods to encourage me to continue.

"I had to get answers, so that's what I did. It took me weeks, but eventually, Brad came around to me. He helped me without ever realizing it."

"What does he think happened?"

"Someone else got blamed for the information leaking. I was an outsider but had covered my tracks."

"Of course."

"Brad will welcome me. He thinks I'm from Las Vegas. That I'm an expert at gambling and beating the odds."

"Are you?"

"I know enough for the jobs I get offered."

"Wait, does this mean that's what you did for his boss? You got in and got the information you needed?"

"I won't lie to you."

"Then don't."

"I'm telling you information on an as-needed basis."

Cara sighs and leans back into the fluffy sofa, frustrated.

"Come on, Sinclair. Where is all that hype saying how great of a contract killer I am?"

"Need to know, Collins."

"Fine, but what would that make you? Some type of card shark?"

She says it almost sarcastically.

"The correct term is 'card sharp,' but card shark has been more widely accepted as of late."

"I don't need a history lesson. A card sharp then?"

"Yes. Card sharp. Card counter. Whatever it takes."

Cara leans forward and mimics my pose of resting her elbows on her knees.

"Seriously?"

"Yes."

"Good to know."

Cara sits upright, and a hint of a smile appears.

"So the man called Ace happens to have all of these card talents?"

"Yes," I groan.

"Hey, I'm not knocking it, but it is a funny coincidence."

"No one has questioned it at least."

"And what about Brad the Bull? His is a funny nickname."

"I wouldn't say that."

Cara gets more serious again.

"How did he get nicknamed the Bull?"

"Destroys everything without question."

"Got it."

Cara soaks in everything I've just shared. I'll give her the space to do so.

"Does he know you're back?"

"Yes. I reached out to him after we got assigned and let him know my new wife and I are settling down in Charlotte, and lo and behold, he's my new neighbor."

"How did he take it?"

"He was surprised. Asked us to stop by at some point, which will be a good setup."

"Very good, actually."

"Why's that?"

"I'm bringing him and his wife a pie tomorrow to say hello."

I smirk as I stretch my neck from side to side.

"You bake pies?" I ask.

"We all have our secret talents."

Cara gets up and leaves me sitting in the living room alone. I watch as she climbs up the stairs to the bedrooms.

I gave her the primary bedroom, and I'll be taking the set-up guest room. It's a way for us to try to keep it professional. At the hotel, it was a nice gesture for her to share the bed with me and nothing more than that.

There wasn't any way I could tell her that I slept well that night for the first time in ages. That normally, my past haunts me in my dreams. That seemed a bit dark for five a.m. over coffee.

"NEVER THOUGHT I'd see the day," I say.

Cara perks up from the oven where she's pulling out a pie.

"It's called homemade."

"I thought you were an order or buy kind of woman."

"I am."

I lean against the nearby counter, cross my arms against my chest, and kick one leg over the other.

"That's for a different phase. This is the 'we're new to the neighborhood and don't know how to fit in' phase."

"Brad knows me."

"And Ace wouldn't have his wife make homemade pies?"

Cara sets down the freshly baked pie next to the others before planting her hands on her hips. A piece of her deep-brown hair falls around her face.

The way the bright-red tank top and short denim shorts she's wearing make her look like any man's housewife wet dream is a disturbing realization.

"Brad will think I'm one lucky bastard to get a wife like you."

Cara smiles, and it's in this moment that I realize I'd like to keep making this woman smile like this.

"Good. Well, I think this is the last one," she says while turning her attention back to the pies.

"How many did you make?" I ask while scanning the pies.

"Just four. For Brad's house, one of the neighbors across the street, the ones on the other side of us, and Ms. Miller down the road."

I uncross my arms and grip the edge of the countertop.

"Why Ms. Miller?"

"Something about her profile just jarred me. I'd like an opportunity to talk to her in person."

"Is that how you'll start the conversation?"

Cara gives me an annoyed look as she shakes her head.

"I think I'll talk to her about anything she wants to talk about. Maybe even the neighborhood painting class she teaches on Thursdays."

"You can paint too?"

"I'm a woman of many talents."

I bet you are.

"You'll bring them over with me still, right?" she asks.

"Of course."

She gives me a small nod as she starts to cover the pies.

"Okay, I'm going to freshen up, and then we can head out."

"You look perfect like that."

Cara grins as I realize what I let slip.

"I mean, perfect for the part."

"Thank you, but I'd rather have my hair down and put on a sundress."

I'd like to pull on that ponytail instead.

"Okay. I'll be down here waiting. Should I bag the pies for you?"

"That'd be great. Thanks!"

Cara walks out of the kitchen, and I hear her going quickly up the stairs. As soon as the bedroom door shuts behind her, I realize I can breathe for the first time. I hadn't intentionally been holding my breath.

I can't let on that I'm coming to terms with the feelings she's stirring up. I have to keep my distance and remain professional. For the sake of the job that just started, my friendship with her dad, and, well, my goddamn dignity.

Getting to work, I stack the covered pies and place them in a warming bag that Cara had laid out.

With the bag prepped, I carry it toward the front door

and wait for Cara. As I take in our new foyer, I hear her coming down the stairs.

Cara emerges around the corner in a green sundress, a tan cardigan, and matching wedges. A far cry from her usual black attire and love of faux leather.

"What do you think?" she asks with a twirl.

"You certainly look the part."

"That's the idea," she says with a smirk.

Cara notices the package of pies I'm holding.

"Want me to get those?"

"That wouldn't be very gentlemanly of me, now would it?"

"I suppose not. Let's start with Brad first?"

"Good idea."

Cara opens the front door and gestures for me to go first. I slip out and wait for her on the picturesque front porch.

"Lead the way, Ace," she teases.

"Let's see how Brad is doing these days."

We walk down the few steps to the ground and then take the sidewalk to the stone path leading right to their front door.

Cara leans in and rings the doorbell and then smooths out the bottom of her dress.

"You look beautiful," I whisper into her ear.

She shivers slightly. I want to take it as a sign she likes when I'm close, but I don't dare think that way.

"Thank you. It's just chilly, so my dress was getting wrinkled."

That feels like a lie, but I won't call her on it.

Suddenly, the door opens wide, and I find Brad's wife, Noelle, standing in the doorway. Her eyes widen in disbelief as they land on me before shooting over to Cara.

"Ace? Is that you?" Noelle asks.

"It is. Did Brad not tell you who your new neighbors are?" I say with a chuckle.

"No, that man certainly did not! Well, come here," she replies.

Noelle widens her arms and steps forward to embrace me. I return her hug, and as we pull away, she holds onto my shoulders for a moment.

"It's great to have you back around."

"Happy to be."

Noelle turns to Cara.

"Don't tell me you married this one?" she teases.

"My own prince charming," Cara jokes back.

"It's lovely to meet you. I'm Noelle. My husband, Brad, is just out back on the grill. Would you two like to come in?"

"We would love to," Cara says before I can.

"Come on in then!"

"This is for you," Cara says as she takes a pie out of the container I'm holding.

Noelle's eyes gleam with delight.

"Ace, you really found a good one, I see."

"The best out there."

Cara smiles warmly at the interaction, and in this moment, even I believe we're a real couple heading to an old friend's house to say hello.

Noelle lets us walk in first and then follows behind with the pie in tow.

"I'm just going to put this in the kitchen. Why don't you both head on out toward the back, and you'll see Brad in a pile of smoke."

Noelle laughs.

"In a way like the old days, right, Ace?"

The memory of the building burning down and me getting Brad out of the fire in time will be imprinted in my mind forever. I left this memory out when talking to Cara, and I'm not really sure why. Brad may have had his suspicions about me, but after that night, he never said a word.

"Right," I murmur.

Cara gives me a side-eye, clearly noticing the change in my tone.

I head out toward the back patio with Cara by my side. She doesn't comment on that exchange.

Opening the sliding glass door, I step out to see the silhouette of a stocky man covered in tattoos behind a smoke-filled grill.

Brad pops his head to the side and must notice our two figures walking onto the patio deck as he closes the grill. The smoke around him starts to dissipate.

"Hi there?" he asks, somewhat questioning who we are still.

"Hi, Brad. It's been a long time."

Brad steps forward, and realization dawns on him that it's me.

"Get over here, you fucker," he jokes.

I close the distance and shake Brad's hand as I balance the bag of pies in the other.

"It's been a while," he says as he lets go of my hand and steps back in amazement.

"I did tell you I'd be coming."

"You did, but that house has been sold for over a month. I didn't know when you'd be moving in."

I glance over to Cara at that bit of news. The agency has owned this house for over a month. They must have been onto Brad in that case. A piece of news they hadn't shared with me at any point. I wonder if they knew about Brad's and my relationship that far in advance and didn't let on.

"You know how it goes. Had to make this one my wife."

Cara beams as she extends her hand out to Brad.

"I'm Cara. It's a pleasure to meet you."

"Cara, the pleasure is mine," he says as he takes her hand in his and places a kiss on top of it.

Cara giggles at the gesture.

"Alright, hands off my woman," I tease.

Brad lets go and brings his hands upward, pretending to be caught.

"First time you've ever raised your hands up like that, mate?"

He lets out a deep, bellowing laugh as he lowers them.

"Don't you know it."

Brad continues to chuckle.

"We're just about to eat some burgers. Interested in staying for a bit?"

"Oh, we wouldn't want to impose," Cara lies.

"Nonsense," Brad says.

Just then, Noelle starts to open the sliding glass door.

"Baby, can you get a couple more burgers?"

"No problem! Do y'all want cheese on them?" she asks.

Cara nods, and I do the same.

"Two cheeseburgers, coming right up," she says before disappearing back inside.

"Thank you," Cara calls out.

"Take a seat." Brad gestures to his patio set.

"Can I get either of you a beer?"

"That'd be great," I answer.

I set down the bag of pies that we still have to share with the other neighbors. Brad walks over to his cooler and pulls out two cans of beer and hands one to each of us.

"Thank you," Cara says.

"Of course."

Brad takes a seat on the opposite side of where Cara and I both sat down.

I crack open my beer, and Cara does the same.

"How has life been, man? What have you been up to?" Brad asks.

"A little this, a little that," I answer.

"Right. Still the same, I see."

"Well, he did also get married," Cara chimes in.

"That he did!" Brad shouts.

Brad focuses his attention on Cara, who is showing off her wedding rings.

"That's a beaut. Looks a lot like the diamonds I've seen recently," he mumbles, almost to himself.

The illegal diamond trade. I don't think Brad intended to say that out loud.

"She deserves the best. How the hell else can someone like me get a girl like this?" I say, trying to distract him.

"I've been asking myself that since she stepped out here next to you," he says with a laugh.

Noelle comes out with the burgers. She walks over to the grill and sets the plate down on the side. Brad gets up to join her there and starts to cook our burgers and plate theirs.

"Thanks for doing this," Cara says.

"Sweetie, of course. We are just so pleased to have y'all here!" Noelle answers.

Brad concentrates on the grill as Noelle takes the two ready burgers and puts them on the patio dining table.

"Do you have plans for this weekend yet? You have to attend the neighborhood barbecue. It'll be a great opportunity to meet everyone."

"When is it?" Cara asks.

"Saturday. One o'clock at Ms. Miller's house right down the road."

"Ms. Miller?"

Noelle's facial expression flusters slightly before going back to her previously friendly demeanor.

"Yes, she basically runs the neighborhood," she answers with a fake laugh.

"She's actually on my list to bring a pie to," Cara says.

"I wouldn't go over there unannounced. If you can bring one on Saturday, I'm sure she would love the gesture."

"We'll do that then. Thank you for the tip," Cara answers.

"Us ladies have to stick together," Noelle says.

"Burgers are ready!" Brad shouts.

"Why don't y'all head over to the dining table? We'll bring your burgers over there."

"Perfect," Cara says.

Cara and I both give each other a knowing look as we walk over to the table as Brad and Noelle focus on the grill.

Noelle is afraid of Ms. Miller, and we need to find out why.

NINE

Grant

"LET'S go over the game plan one last time," Cara says.

She's standing in the kitchen looking at the apple crumble pie she's baked for the party. One for Ms. Miller and the other for guests.

"Yes, boss."

Cara looks over her shoulder and gives me a pointed stare. I can't help but chuckle as I walk around the island to where she is.

She's been every bit the serious woman I had gotten to know during our run-ins. It doesn't help that I can't be in her proximity without my cock reacting.

"I'm serious."

"I know, but we have the plan down."

"Okay, so tell me it."

She stacks the now-covered pies and slips them into the same case we had used earlier in the week. We got to meet the other neighbors surrounding us as planned.

"We're arriving fifteen minutes late on purpose. We'll find Brad and Noelle, who will be on time. We'll put the pie down with the other dishes and then go and find this elusive Ms. Miller."

Cara nods along as she walks past me and toward the living room. I follow behind, like I've been doing a lot lately.

"After meeting Ms. Miller, we'll say hello to the neighbors we've met who are also coming. Meet a few new faces, and then I'll corner Brad."

"We need to get into that casino."

"As friendlies."

"Right."

Cara sets down the pie bag on the entryway table and looks around the room. She swishes her shoulders excitedly in triumph for spotting her wedges.

Picking them up, she sits down on the couch and starts to put them on.

"It was a good catch during our surveillance."

"An easy spot. You probably would have too."

"True..."

Cara peers over her shoulder and smiles.

"Eventually," she teases.

"Ouch, you wound me," I say with a hand over my heart.

She lets out a light laugh as she finishes buckling the last shoe.

"An underground casino for the wealthy. Makes sense they finally made it official."

"Yeah, you mentioned last time it wasn't under the Carolinas mafia, right?"

"Right. Well, not officially. Not like this."

"It's been some time. Makes sense with all the expansion into different trades they've been getting into the past couple of years."

Cara gets up and walks over to where I'm waiting with the pies in hand.

"Ready?" she asks.

"Ready."

MS. MILLER'S house is one of the largest in the neighborhood, potentially the most acreage, at least with the size of this backyard.

I laugh to myself. Calling this a backyard doesn't do it justice.

The back gate was left open for guests to enter through. There are dozens of people dressed like they all just came out of a catalog. With bright colors everywhere, it's as if they match the tropical greenery of the yard.

It's flawless.

"Are you thinking what I am?" Cara asks as we simultaneously spot a large spread of food.

We both start walking in that direction to set down the pie, a gesture for the party that won't go unnoticed as the two outsiders here.

"Brad and Noelle are over there," I whisper.

Cara's eyes dart over to where I'm subtly gesturing. She spots them talking to one of the neighbors we brought a pie over to earlier this week, Fred. He's a single man who lives in a house that looks to be the same model as ours.

"Let's go," she says.

We walk across the wooden deck and down the other set of steps. Brad spots us and waves us over. Cara gives him one of her breathtaking smiles, and a sting of jealousy courses through me.

I pause to compose myself. There's nothing to be jealous of because Cara isn't mine.

"You okay?" she whispers as we continue forward.

"All good."

I keep hold of the last pie as we close the remaining distance.

Who would have guessed I would be thinking about pies this much? Certainly not me in this lifetime.

"Hey there!" Cara beams.

"Hi!" Noelle responds as she gives Cara a side hug. They step to the side and start chatting about how our move-in is going.

"Good to see you could make it," Brad says.

"Wouldn't miss it."

He looks over to Fred.

"Have you had a chance to meet Ace yet?"

"Earlier this week," he answers before turning his attention to me.

"Is that one of your wife's pies?"

"It is," I say, showcasing it.

"What I wouldn't give for another taste of your wife's pie." He flashes me a smug smile.

I clear my throat and clench my jaw.

Cara isn't baking pies for him anymore.

"This one is for Ms. Miller. Anyone know where she is?" I say loud enough to get Noelle and Cara's attention.

"Brad, sweetie, why don't you take them to her?" Noelle says.

Her tone said everything we needed it to; Noelle isn't comfortable around Ms. Miller, and I think it's because she's the Kingpin of Charlotte. The one who's closest to the Marlin's operations locally.

Brad's face falls briefly, but he quickly collects himself.

"Right this way. Last time I saw her, she was inside with some of the other guests."

Brad doesn't wait for either of us to answer as he turns on his heels and starts going up the stairs.

"We'll be back," Cara says.

"See you soon!" Noelle answers.

Cara holds onto one of my arms as we follow behind Brad up the deck and into Ms. Miller's home.

"We've got this," Cara says.

"I know."

Cara tries to examine my expression for any sign of discomfort, but what she needs to realize is this has been my job for almost thirty years. I'll never let her see any of that.

I'm not nervous to meet this Ms. Miller character. The comment Fred made is really irritating me instead.

What was that about? Testing me. He must be someone in the mafia or related to think he could make a comment like that to me, and I would stand down.

The chances are that he is just a prick with a small dick, but it's possible he's something more in the operation. I'll have to investigate him further after this. I can't let my complicated feelings for my partner disrupt any part of the plan.

"She's right over here," Brad says.

In the corner across the formal living room, near a set of closed double wooden doors, is the elusive Ms. Miller.

It has to be.

Surrounded by what are clearly her guards, she's engaging with a couple who looks like they probably live in our neighborhood.

She's a fit woman, proudly showcasing her physique in a pair of tiny white shorts and a tank top. With her long, billowing blonde and gray hair, I'd guess she's in her fifties, most likely.

What I don't spot is a companion of any kind nearby. She's been introduced to us as Miss and not Mrs. Miller, which could suggest she's single or has a partner but isn't married.

It could go either way if my theory is correct about who she really is.

Brad tilts his head forward, encouraging us to come up to where he stands. I adjust the pie bag in my hands as Cara's grip tightens on my arm.

"Here we go," she says through a strained smile.

Brad focuses his attention on Ms. Miller, who has realized that he's waiting outside of her guarded perimeter. She looks around and notices that Cara and I are standing with him as well.

"Bradley! Come in here," she exclaims.

I watch as she says her goodbye to the other couple before they step out of the area and disappear entirely.

"And who might you have with you?" she asks as we all step into her space.

"Ms. Miller, this is Ace and Cara Weston, my new neighbors," Brad says.

"It is a pleasure to meet you," Cara says.

"Isn't this wonderful! The pleasure is all mine. I'm Cordelia Miller. Welcome to the neighborhood," Cordelia says with her arms extended.

Cara and Cordelia share a cautious hug as if this were any other set of neighbors meeting for the first time.

As they pull away, Cordelia gets a twinkle in her eye as she turns her attention my way.

"And it's a pleasure to finally meet you, Ace," she says with her hand extended. I pass our pie bag to Cara and then take her hand immediately, giving it a firm shake.

Cordelia looks pleased with this development. It's almost as if Brad had told her who I was and that I would be moving to Charlotte soon.

I'm making some assumptions, but it feels as if our plans are falling into place.

The way that Cordelia is eyeing me isn't one of seduction but appraisal. I'm almost positive that she's the Kingpin of Charlotte that Cara has been trying to track down.

"Thank you for the invitation to attend. We brought you one of my famous pies," Cara says.

Cordelia doesn't look back over to Cara.

"Well, isn't that the sweetest, sugar. Thank you."

Cordelia lets go of my hand and leans back to whisper something to one of her guards. He takes the pie bag out of Cara's hands.

"What would you like to drink? Drew here can grab us a round."

"Whatever you're having," Cara says.

"Sugar, you like a whiskey neat?"

Cordelia may have had plastic surgery to try and hide her age, but I can see the hint of exhaustion and boredom in her eyes.

"Love it."

"I'll be damned. Four whiskeys, Drew."

"Coming right up."

Drew heads toward the bar, and someone else immediately steps in to fill the half circle around Cordelia.

"How are y'all settling into the neighborhood?"

"It's breathtaking," Cara answers.

"It really is. One of a kind neighborhood. We're all..." Cordelia trails off before looking over to Brad.

"Like a family."

"That's exactly what we want. I'm so glad that Ace was able to find us a home here," Cara says.

"Then you'll fit right in. Either you fit into the Rippling River community, or you don't. I hate to be frank about that, but it is what it is."

"Hopefully we will," Cara says while keeping her smile firmly intact.

It's almost disturbing how Cara is able to keep this fake smile in place. If she weren't a practiced spy, I would be alarmed at how well she's playing this role.

"Ace, I hear you and Bradley go way back."

"We do."

Cordelia studies me once again.

"Good. A friend of Bradley's is always a friend of mine."

"I hope I won't let you down."

"I have a feeling you won't. I tend to be right about people."

Drew appears and hands Cordelia her drink first before handing the rest of ours out. Cara, Brad, and I all share our thanks.

"To new and old friends," Cordelia says with a raised glass in the air.

"Cheers."

We all down the whiskey as if they were shots. Cordelia notices that we fell in line, and a pleased expression takes over.

"Good. Now, who wants to challenge me in a little cornhole game? I absolutely love it," she says.

"Then we should be on a team because I always beat Ace," Cara says with a giggle.

"Cara's on my team! Ace, Bradley, you can be our challengers."

We all laugh and start to head out back. Cordelia has Cara's arm in hers and begins telling her details about the architecture of the house as they walk through it. The sea of people naturally parts as they do. Another sign that Cordelia holds an important role here.

I look over to Brad, who has a light sheen covering his skin.

"Everything okay?" I ask.

"I'm glad that went well."

"Me too," I add, pretending to feign confusion. "Were you worried it wouldn't?"

"Another time, Ace."

"Why won't you tell me what's going on?"

"Not everything is what it seems."

"Whatever you say."

Catching up to Cara, I pull her aside.

"Are you really good at cornhole?" I ask.

"Another special talent," Cara whispers.

"You're full of hidden talents."

"I did grow up in a small town. It's not hard to fathom that I would know how to bake or play some yard games."

"I suppose that's true."

Cara peers up at me through her long eyelashes, making me wish the look in her eyes was real. She grazes her hand against my chest before resting it there.

"Maybe one day you'll find out about more of them."

I feel the exuding heat between us, and I'll be damned, but I wish it was real and not for show. All eyes are on us as we wait for the cornhole boards to be set up.

"I already know that you, my lucky charm, are anything but predictable. I'm not sure why your hidden suburban talents have come as a shock. I'll rectify my reactions immediately," I murmur.

"Good. I wouldn't take you for someone who couldn't handle what I can dish out."

"Believe me, I can."

Cara stands up on the balls of her feet and opens her mouth to speak as she grips onto my shoulders to steady her balance. I can feel her breath teasing my lips, and I want to devour them whole right here in front of everyone.

As her husband, it would make sense that I do. My only problem is that I want to kiss her without it being a spectacle.

"Promises, promises," she murmurs.

Cara places a soft kiss on my lips, and it sends a jolt of electricity through my body. This is the second time we've kissed, and both times, I've had a visceral reaction to the way she tastes.

"Oh boy, it's getting hot in here," Cordelia taunts.

Cara steps to the side but stays latched onto me and grins.

"We are newlyweds," she says with a giggle.

"Newlyweds! I had no idea. Congratulations are in order," Cordelia shouts.

"Thank you," I answer.

Cordelia places her hands on her hips and cocks a leg out to the side.

"You know what? Why don't you two come to my casino? We have a special tournament next week. Invite only. You two can be my special guests."

"That would be wonderful," Cara exclaims.

"You like to gamble?"

"I love it. I'm not an expert, but I can hold my own."

"Alright, between you and Ace playing, maybe we'll have a show after all," Cordelia says with a chuckle.

"Let's see if you're as good as you say you are at cornhole first."

"You know it."

Cara leaves my side and heads to the opposite board that Cordelia is waiting by.

"Boys, why don't you two sit this one out? Two of the other women wanted to play."

"Of course, ladies first," I answer ahead of Brad.

He gives a slight nod and then walks over to where I stand.

The game gets started, and I can sense by the way Brad is fidgeting that something is up. He's either uncomfortable that I got an invite so soon, or there's a different matter he's itching to tell me. It must have something to do with why he was being so cryptic earlier. Either way, I can't make the first move and ask about the casino night.

We got an invite from the woman of the hour. It's the best luck we could have had with this case so early on.

Brad crosses his arms against his chest.

"She knows about you."

"What about me?"

"Your past."

I cross my arms to mimic his pose.

"Will that be a problem? I don't count cards anymore."

He laughs in disbelief.

"You don't get it."

"No, I don't. Why don't you tell me?"

Brad faces me and uncrosses his arms. He stuffs them in his pockets as he rocks on his heels.

"Ms. Miller," he starts.

Brad clears his throat.

"Cordelia, I should say."

"Yeah?"

"She's got connections around here. Is this the life you want back into? Is this why you became my fucking neighbor, Ace? You gotta tell me. I can't help you if I don't know what you're doing here."

"I want the best life possible for my new wife."

Brad nods as he considers my confession.

"She'll want you to count cards Thursday."

"Why?"

"Outside of the obvious, to make her money," he begins.

"Yeah?"

"Because it's more than a game to her. It's part of how she operates."

"Does she own the casino?"

Brad lets out a long sigh.

"Come on, Ace. I know you know she does. It's obvious what's happening here."

I won't disagree, but I need him to say it.

"She's auditioning you."

"To work for her at the casino?"

"Not like some dead-end job, man. She knows who you are, and she collects the best in the Carolinas."

"That would make her..."

"I'm not going to say it."

"Let's go with important."

"Yes."

"Then I better show her my cards on Thursday."

TEN

Cara

STARING at the note that Grant left me once again, I'm getting nervous for our night in together. He's going to be teaching me some of his card tricks. Neither of us thinks that Cordelia will expect me to be as proficient as he is, but I need to have some understanding of gambling.

Even though Grant and I are newlyweds, we would have been dating for some time ahead of getting married. It would make sense that I would understand the games that afford us this lifestyle.

Growing up in Massachusetts, I had a core group of friends that I spent all my time with: Lachlan, Grayson, and Liam. They used to play cards together periodically, but I never found it interesting.

Since I was always by their sides, I would be pulled into a few rounds to make the stakes more interesting or listen to their conversations about it. Right now, I'm happy I didn't just ignore them like I did with other topics I found dull.

When Grant asked if I had a basic understanding of how to play a few games, I was able to be honest with him when I said yes. I probably would have lied to anyone else if I didn't, but I'd rather not lie to Grant.

An air of mystery surrounds the man, and there is so much about his past that I have yet to learn. Especially when it comes to his time with Brad.

My gut is telling me that there's more to the story and that Grant is hiding some of his past from me. But for now, I'm going to keep trusting him at face value.

Truthfully, I have no other choice but to trust the man who holds the cards to bring down the Kingpin.

I shake my head in disbelief.

Cordelia is the Kingpin. I need to wrap my head around the fact that this figure I've been chasing for years is masquerading as this pleasant suburban woman. I know the Kingpin as a ruthless killer and operator of illegal trading and not this.

It takes everything in me to not arrest her immediately for her crimes, but the Kingpin is no longer my primary target—the Marlin is.

Pulling out a sleek black dress, I slip it on over my head and examine myself in the mirror. It's short with a slightly plunging neckline and will be the perfect look for tonight.

Maybe that's overtly confident of me to wear tonight, but I want to impress Grant. We've been here now for a week, and he hasn't so much as looked at me the way he had before the barbecue at Cordelia's house.

The feeling of being roommates and partners only has been wearing on me. I'm well aware that's all we are, but I just want to feel that spark one more time.

There's so much unanswered by him, and I still don't know why, after years of torment, I want him to notice me.

The short truth is that I want his attention.

I want Grant to see me fully.

I want to be wanted by the man shrouded in mystery.

I'm beginning to crave Grant Sinclair.

Is that such a bad desire to have? I certainly hope not; otherwise, the next few weeks are going to continue to go by at a snail's pace. What we thought was going to take months could really only be a few weeks.

Cordelia's invitation to the tournament was unexpected, but Grant's past as Ace was too tempting for her to pass up.

Walking down the stairs, I try to exude confidence in case Grant is already back from the store. He didn't share why he was going, but I imagine it has something to do with this evening.

I descend the staircase and head toward the living room to look for Grant.

That's when I pause midstep.

A soft glow is coming from the room. Slowly, I keep going forward, wondering what's happening in there.

When I finally see what it is, I can't believe my eyes. My heart feels like it's going to jump out of my chest.

Grant is tending to the fireplace, wearing a pair of dark-washed jeans and a white collared shirt with the sleeves rolled up. Even with his back to me, he's every bit as delicious-looking as he normally is.

That's when I notice the dozens of candles spread throughout the room. There's a charcuterie board on the coffee table and two glasses of red wine sitting next to it. Centered is a deck of cards and a poker case.

"No poker table? I'm shocked," I say.

Grant's back vibrates slightly, and I call that a victory. I got the man to laugh again, a small win that I'm collecting.

"I did think about it, but I figured it might be too much."

He faces me with a wide smile that makes me want to drop this façade altogether and tell him we should stop pretending while we're living together like this.

I glance around the room once more.

"What a setup. Have a date after you teach me poker?"

Grant's smile is devilish as he tilts his head to the side and places his hands in his pockets.

"All for you."

"What a waste," I say.

His smile drops, and I realize if I want to show him what I want, then I need to stop the comebacks.

"Sorry. Old habits die hard," I add.

That smile reappears, and he nods in acceptance.

"Glass of wine?"

"Is it poisoned?" I tease.

"No, love. I'd like to keep you around."

Love. Not darling like he usually calls me.

I shouldn't let that word have any more meaning than how he probably meant it. Just another term of endearment he would use with anyone he's partnered with.

Heading around the couch, I settle down on the open space in front of the coffee table. Grant notices and sits down too.

He hands me the glass of wine, and I watch as he drinks in my outfit. I love being under his gaze. The dress was the right call.

"I like the dress of choice."

"I knew you would."

I take a sip of the wine as Grant picks up his glass.

"No toast? Bad form, Collins."

"I certainly do apologize, Sinclair."

Grant takes a sip of his wine.

"You can make it up to me."

"How would I ever do that?"

"I'm sure we can think of something."

"Whatever you say."

Grant hums thoughtfully.

"You said you've played poker before, correct?"

"Yes."

"How much?"

"Honestly?" I ask as I swirl my wine around in its glass.

"I'd appreciate it, given the stakes."

"Back home in Massachusetts. My friends would play, and I'd be forced into it."

"Friends?"

"I'm sure you've heard my dad talk about them. Lachlan, Grayson, and Liam. From Hull."

"That's right. You four are still close, correct?"

"Yes, well, it's complicated. I am friends with all of them."

Grant doesn't press any further, which I appreciate. A long time ago, we all had a falling out over a misunderstanding. Grayson and I talk to everyone, but Lachlan and Liam still aren't speaking to one another.

It's something that Grayson and I plan to team up and resolve after I'm done with this mission.

"It explains a lot."

"What does?"

"Your loyalty."

I shrug, trying to stay indifferent even though Grant is getting to know me on a more personal level.

"How so?"

"Come on, Cara. There's no need to hide. Not with me."

"Isn't that basically what we are doing together? Hiding?"

"We aren't hiding. We're the good guys."

I let out a light laugh, and it makes Grant move closer in my direction.

"We are."

Grant's stare is intense on me.

"You're talented. Loyal. Confident. Have one hell of a shot and the looks to bring any of these fuckers to their knees."

I feign confusion.

"Which shot are you referring to?"

Grant smirks.

"Fine, all your shots are good."

"That's better."

"And funny."

"Wow, maybe I'll have to make you my real husband."

Grant's jaw ticks as he looks away.

"Kidding. Don't worry, I'm a professional," I tease.

Grant's eyes find mine, and there's a hint of something in them that I can't quite make out. I'm meant to be reading people and situations at an expert level, but I suppose Grant is used to masking the real him.

"Hey, Grant?"

"Yeah?"

"Thank you. All of that was really nice to hear."

"It's true."

"You know, you aren't so bad yourself."

He laughs.

"I don't know about that."

"Fishing for a compliment?"

"No, I've just lived a lot of life. Not sure how I ended

up here, but I'm glad I get to pretend to have a life like this with you."

My heart flutters.

"Where you get involved with the mafia?" I joke.

"Exactly."

We're both smiling from ear to ear now, and suddenly, I realize that maybe Grant likes spending time with me too.

"Ready to learn how to play poker first?"

"Ready," I say with a salute.

"Okay, let's get started."

Grant picks up the cards and shuffles them before passing them out. He gives me a quick reminder of the rules, and before long, we're in our first game.

"I want to start with the basics tonight. Tomorrow, we can go over some of my tricks."

"I thought we were doing that tonight?"

Grant looks up from his cards and grins.

"I think I want another night alone with my wife."

I FIND myself once again standing in front of my full-length mirror, about to go downstairs to spend another intimate evening with Grant. One where I'll get to know more about his background through little tidbits he'll share.

I know tonight is also where my feelings will get even more complicated for the man after our previous night together.

I had gone into last night wanting to show myself off to him a bit, and boy, did that backfire. Not only did I show myself off, but Grant apparently liked it but respected our boundaries.

It was infuriating.

Respect.

Maybe I just wanted to be manhandled? But Mr. Charming wasn't going to do that. Not with me.

So tonight, I plan to take things one step further. After he teaches me a few secrets of his trade, I'm going to talk to him about us practicing being more intimate for our appearance tomorrow night at the casino.

Usually, I'm very confident, but with our walls crumbling, I wonder if I'll be able to muster up the courage. Somehow, Grant sees past every façade I put up, and we're just getting to know each other.

It should make me feel uneasy, but it doesn't.

I just need to know if our feelings align. I know with one touch, I'll be able to tell if the man is truly interested in me or if I'm just some type of potential convenience.

Heading downstairs, I'm greeted by a familiar sight. Candles are lit around the room, and a handsome man waits for me at the bottom of the steps.

This has to mean something. I need to either ask him what parts of this are real or just let it go.

"You look beautiful," Grant says as he takes my hand in his.

"Thank you."

Heading into the living room, I see it's set up once more to rival the other night.

I look up at Grant and see a twinkle of something in his eyes that I've only caught on the rare occasion.

"Why are you doing all this?" I ask.

"Have a seat," he says to avoid the question.

Just like before, I take a seat on the floor in front of the coffee table, and he does the same. I pick up the glass of red wine waiting for me.

It's a similar routine that I want to become a tradition between us, but I can't possibly tell the man.

"What are we starting with tonight?" I ask.

Taking a sip, I watch as Grant carefully studies my mouth. Putting on a bit of a playful show, I pull the glass away and lick my bottom lip as I set the glass down.

"Delicious choice," I add.

Grant clears his throat and picks up the deck of cards.

"Blackjack."

"Great."

I straighten my shoulders as Grant starts setting up.

"Remember the rules?"

"How can I forget the rules of the game?"

His eyes snap to mine momentarily.

"Good."

He takes a sip of his own drink and sets it back down on the table.

"Cordelia won't expect you to know everything. We'll make it clear that you and I met through the circles if needed, but you aren't a card expert."

"Right."

"She will expect you to have a basic understanding of how counting cards works."

"That's not something everyone can do?"

Grant laughs lightly.

"No, love. That's not something everyone can do and certainly not well."

There's that nickname again.

"As long as I'm not expected to know how to do it well in this time frame."

"Someone like you will have no issue picking up this skill. Watch."

My heart flutters from the compliment, but I don't show any reaction. He's right; someone in my line of work and at the caliber he and I operate should have no issue picking this up.

I shouldn't be taking it as a compliment specific to me as a person. It's my job to learn things like this quickly.

"Okay, ready to watch and learn."

"YOU DID REALLY WELL. I'm just as impressed as I knew I would be," he says.

We're both sitting on the couch after hours of him running through counting cards, mucking cards at poker, and other tricks.

"Thank you," I say with a sigh.

"Tired?"

"A bit. It was all good to know. It's just..."

Grant lets his arm leaning at the top of the couch fall, and his fingers graze the tip of mine.

"It's what?"

"I get that in our line of work, we deal with these types of people. It just seems like all of this is more work than becoming proficient at playing the different card games, that's all."

Grant pulls his arm back slightly.

"You're not wrong about that."

"But, I know this is the surefire way to win. And that's all they're thinking about."

"Especially when you play in casinos like the ones Cordelia owns."

"Right."

I chew on my bottom lip.

"What's wrong?"

"She's an interesting one. I wouldn't have assumed the person I was chasing all this time would be her. She just doesn't fit the profile of the Kingpin I've been trying to find."

Grant nods in understanding.

"Sometimes the profiles are wrong. That's why it's good we're here in the field. When we go to her casino, we'll get the confirmation we need."

"And hopefully find out more about the operation."

"All in due time."

I pick up my wine glass and get comfortable on the couch once more.

"I know this takes time, but I've been tracking her for ages. I just want this win so badly."

"You'll get it. Once we're in and part of the family, as they say, we'll get more access than we could dream of right now."

"We need to scope it out when we go."

"We will. I promise."

I know we should probably head to bed, but I want to keep chatting with Grant. I'm suddenly not feeling as courageous as I was at the start, but I still long to be around him. I don't want to go back to my empty bedroom alone.

"Can I ask you a question?" he asks.

"Yeah, sure."

He doesn't want it to end either.

"Why the Kingpin of Charlotte? I've never been able to figure it out."

"Are you telling me that I've stumped the great Grant Sinclair on something?" I tease.

"Maybe you have."

I blush into my shoulder.

"It's a long story."

"We have time."

"One of my best friends, Liam, has a sister, Harper. She's now engaged to Grayson."

"Brother's best friend? How forbidden," Grant says with a chuckle.

Not as forbidden as if I slept with my dad's best friend like I want to, but I won't bring that up.

"She's younger than us by a few years and had a terrible ex-boyfriend. Anyhow, that ex-boyfriend was one of the Kingpin's, I mean, Cordelia's runners."

Grant focuses on this news.

"Yeah. I thought it was a man for a long time, but until recently, I wasn't positive. The profiles, as you know, can vary with new intel. Anyway, the ex-boyfriend really scared Harper. That's why I got involved, and then, well, it was too good of a case to pass up."

"You did this on your own."

"Yeah, no one hired me to track down the Kingpin, really. It's been a passion project of mine."

"I can understand how that goes."

"The Marlin."

He sighs.

"Yeah, the Marlin."

"The two of us are something else," I say with a light laugh.

A yawn takes over, and I cover my mouth with the hand not holding my wine glass before shaking out of my tired state.

"Let's get to bed. It's been a long few days."

"How did it go with Brad this morning? It totally slipped my mind."

Grant grabs his wine glass and takes a sip. I take a drink, too, forgetting I hadn't a few moments ago.

"Noelle was around, so he wouldn't get into it."

"Noelle knows something but not everything."

"I'm not sure what her angle is. Was Brad acting as if she wasn't a player this go around? Possibly. When we're at the tournament, we'll know for sure."

"She was before?"

"Yes and no. She was but barely. It's when she and Brad were just getting together. She was around but not fully in, from what I could tell."

"Is that the angle we're taking with me?"

Grant looks aghast at my question.

"You're my wife, Cara. Not a piece of ass I'm getting to know."

I rear my head back.

"I know that. But even with our fake profiles and takes, we have to be clear about my role."

Grant hangs his head back and runs his hand down the length of his face.

"We've been putting it on the back burner until you had more time to talk to Brad. Doesn't seem like Brad is being very helpful."

"You're my wife. We met in Las Vegas. Then it's just your cover from there."

"Right. A few break-ins and cons."

"That's right. You're gorgeous, and it's an easy sell."

"Thank you. Hopefully it is."

"I know it will be."

I set my glass down.

"There's another thing we haven't discussed. Well, not exactly."

"What's that?"

Heat starts to rise in my cheeks, like a schoolgirl talking

to a crush and not a security expert talking to her partner on a case.

"We haven't talked about being intimate in public. We made it through the barbecue with only a quick kiss. It's strange if we don't do anything together while we're around other people."

"We'll play it by ear."

I sigh.

"That's not very professional. We need to know each other's boundaries."

The tension between us is thick.

"What if I don't want to be very professional with you?" He asks.

I gasp and fling a hand over my open mouth. Grant's posture tightens as a tick in his jaw flexes.

"A joke, Collins."

I lower my hand and place both of them in my lap.

"Didn't seem like a joke to me."

"It was."

Grant looks down at his watch.

"It's late. I think it's time we call it a night this time," he says.

"Grant..."

He sighs and then stands. With an outstretched hand to me, Grant grins.

"It was a joke, Collins. Don't worry; I think you and I will be just fine on that front."

"Okay," I lie as I place my hand in his.

This song and dance will resume another night, but I don't think I can let it continue forever.

I want Grant, only I need to know where he stands. And more importantly, I need to know about our pasts in order to attempt a future.

ELEVEN

Grant

TO SAY Cara Collins has successfully messed with my head would be an understatement.

I'm not quite sure how this woman has gotten under my skin like she has, but I know I have to keep her at arm's length. Ordinarily, I would have given in a lot sooner than this. The amount of blue balls this woman has given me is obscene, and she has no idea what she's doing to me.

If this were anyone else, I would have left for a day to find a sexual partner out of state to help distract me from my situation, but alas, it's not.

Instead, it's the woman who has been distracting me for years.

This isn't some flippant crush on a partner or someone I've come across a time or two; it's Cara. The woman who has been haunting me day and night. The one I promised myself to protect. The one whom I can now admit the truth about.

She's the woman I'm falling in love with.

It's pathetic.

I can't find love at my age with someone like Cara. I see the way she looks at me, longingly and with lust in her eyes. There's no way that what she feels is real. It has to be because she hasn't had sex either in the past couple of weeks.

When did I start caring about feelings all the time? I'm a shell of the man I was before this mission started. This woman has made me a complete and utter mess, and I'm the fool who thought that making her my wife on paper would help the matter.

If anything, it's made her crawl under my skin more than ever before. All it takes is a whiff of her perfume or watching her study a file for hours, and I'm turned on.

Even her taking lead on the calls with Dodger has me falling more for this woman than I thought possible.

I should be paying attention to what Cara's telling Dodger during this check-in call, but instead, I'm daydreaming about the way her mouth moves as she speaks with ease to him. She's confident and sure of herself as she explains what we've found already and our upcoming plans.

I know there's something between the two of them. Not a present matter but something of the past.

"Sir, we attend tonight," she finishes.

"That's excellent news, Collins," he answers.

"Anything to add, Sinclair?" Cara asks.

"Well said. Tonight is the first time we'll be in the Kingpin's secret hideout. Nothing more to report until tomorrow."

"Very well," Dodger says.

He pauses on the video monitor. Normally, Dodger isn't

one to mince words, so it makes me feel uneasy that he's debating something.

"Report back to me tomorrow."

"Will do," Cara answers for us.

She shuts the laptop screen down and turns her attention toward me.

"So quiet."

"You had it covered."

Cara twitches her lips for a moment.

"You did," I continue.

"Okay. Whatever you say."

Right as I'm about to ask her about Dodger, our front doorbell rings.

"I'll get it," I say as a way to leave the table.

Sliding out of the kitchen nook, I head into the living room toward the front door. As I'm about to answer it, the doorbell rings through the house once again.

I square my shoulders back and open the door. To my surprise, it's Brad.

"Nice to see you, man. What's going on?" I ask.

"We need to talk," he says while looking from side to side.

"Everything okay?"

I notice his hands are in the front pockets of his pants, and he's twitching more than usual.

"Can I come in?"

"Sure," I answer as I gesture for him to walk through.

He does and immediately helps me shut the door behind him.

"What's going on?" I ask.

"Is everything okay?" Cara calls out.

"All good, love. It's just Brad. He and I will be a few minutes in here."

Cara comes out from the kitchen with a wide smile on her face.

"Brad. So good to see you. Can I get you anything to drink?"

"No, thank you," he says as he scratches his neck.

"Okay, I'll just be upstairs getting ready for tonight. I have to check in with my friend Ruby about some things too," Cara says.

"Tell Ruby hello. Maybe she can fill our friend Rob in as well?"

"No problem. I'll tell her to talk to Rob about how the move-in has been going."

I see the slight furrow between her eyebrows as she takes in Brad's peculiar demeanor.

She looks up at me, and I give her a reassuring signal. Cara and I have taken to being able to say so much without saying anything at all to one another.

As Cara heads up the stairs, I look at how Brad is pacing around the room.

"Take a seat," I say.

"Thanks," he answers, almost relieved.

Brad sits down in the closest seat, a lone accent chair. I sit on the main sofa nearby.

"You don't look so good," I say.

Brad breathes out a long rush of air.

"This is the one favor I'm going to do for you since you are so adamant about getting involved here."

"Okay..."

Brad rests his hands on top of his bouncing knees.

"If you say I told you, I'll lie. Got it?"

"Yes."

I sit still as I wait for Brad to share.

"This is bigger than anything I've been involved with, Ace."

"How so?"

"It's not just local or even, fuck, just the Carolinas. This goes bigger than cards and drugs."

"What is it?"

"This is *it*."

"That's not telling me much."

I need him to share more. We already assume that Cordelia is the Kingpin we've been waiting to get. I need more than this.

"There are big players coming to the tournament tonight. Cordelia's tournament is the place to be."

"In what way?"

"Ace. I like you. Your wife seems like good people too."

"Brad, I saved your life."

"And this isn't the time you want to play that card. You only get it once from me."

I hang my head as I grip the edge of the couch.

"You gotta give me more than that."

"The Marlin."

My head shoots up to find Brad's weary expression on mine.

"Are you sure?"

"This tournament is one of many. Cordelia is auditioning you for more than you know. The Marlin trades in drugs, diamonds, everything but people and kids. Says everyone needs a code."

"A code?"

"A moral one, if you can believe that," he says in disbelief.

"At least we know that much about the Marlin."

Brad's expression turns more serious.

"No one knows anything real about the Marlin. Remember that before tonight."

"I will. Have you met the Marlin before?"

"I can't answer that."

"Why?"

"I'm not telling you more than I can to feel safe. You want in this mess? Then you need to figure it out as you go. But Ace?"

I wait for him to continue.

"Nothing is what it seems. Don't come to this game unless you really understand that."

"I do. Thank you for coming here."

Brad gets up and leaves without another word.

If what he's saying is true, then tonight is the night that Cara and I have to try and figure out who the Marlin is and how everyone is connected.

We need to know from Cordelia what the big play is and when it's happening to put an end to this once and for all. The sooner that we catch the Marlin, the sooner I can retreat back to California and figure out my life.

It's pathetic.

I'm the closest I've ever been to meeting the Marlin, and all I can think about is the way Cara glances at me. If this isn't a sign that I have to figure out my life after this, then I don't know what is.

What we thought was going to take months still could, but less than two weeks in, and we're already heading to the casino as friends of Cordelia's. That'll show all the players we don't know are involved that we can be trusted or, at the very least, are important enough.

I head up the stairs, finding Cara's door slightly ajar. She's examining herself in the mirror. With long cascading locks rolling down her back and a different black sequin dress on, she looks every bit the part that we need her to play.

That's the problem.

The more I see her like this, the more I want her for my own.

I don't just want the happy housewife; I want the vixen I know is underneath those clothes. The one who puts me in my place when necessary and softens when I need that too.

And most importantly, I want to be that person for Cara in return. The one her father, Luke, described would be best for Cara. I could be her partner in every way imaginable if only things were different between us.

Cara glances over her shoulder, and our eyes meet. She tries to turn around to face me, but I'm gone before she can ask me what I was doing or how the conversation with Brad turned out.

In my room, I quickly change into my tuxedo. These tuxedos are beginning to feel like a second skin with the rate I'm wearing them. In my day-to-day life, I don't usually dress this formal, despite what Cara may think.

If Cordelia is hosting a big tournament at the casino, then this will be one of the events where all the local who's who will be. Never mind all our neighbors in Rippling River, but throughout the Carolinas as well.

That reminds me, I need to ask Fisher if he's gotten any word of it down in Charleston.

Picking up my phone off the dresser, I shoot him a quick and discreet text message. Ever since Fisher has been in Charleston, he's been running with a local crowd, where surely this would have made its way to them.

Charlotte, North Carolina, and Charleston, South Carolina, are only about a four- or five-hour drive apart. For

Americans, driving that distance is an easy road trip. Or they could take a flight that's under an hour to get here. That's also a possibility for the elite to do without a care in the world.

"Knock, knock," Cara says as she taps her knuckles against my open bedroom door.

"Almost ready."

Cara walks closer until I can feel the heat of her body only mere inches away.

"Need help?" Her voice comes out sultry, almost as if it were unintended.

I don't, but I turn as I place the bow tie around my neck. She puts her hands on my chest and peers up at me.

"May I?"

"Be my guest," I whisper.

Her delicate fingers tease the length of mine as they pass by one another. She takes the end of the bow tie in her hands as mine fall to my side.

As she finishes, she gives the ends a tight pull and drops her hands to her sides. Cara's breath becomes uneven, and she doesn't step away.

"Grant," she murmurs.

I swallow thickly as I place a hand gently on one of her hips. Cara lets out a soft moan that makes me want to say fuck all the rules and take her right now as mine.

Fuck the tournament.

Fuck catching the Marlin.

Fuck all the preconceived notions that I had about why she and I can't ever be together.

"Cara," I rasp.

She grips onto my shoulders and finally gazes up at me.

"What are we doing?"

"Pretending."

"What if I don't want to pretend with you?" she asks.

My heart sinks momentarily until I realize what she's really saying.

The conviction in her eyes is almost all the confirmation I need to know that we are on the same page.

"I don't want to pretend with you while we're here, Grant. *Please*," she says.

Fuck.

While we're here.

This is all temporary to her, as I knew it would be. I can't take the risk that's involved if this is temporary. Not only for my old heart but because of everything else that's at stake.

My head hangs low, and our foreheads touch one another. Our breathing is heavy, but I have to be the one to put a stop to it.

Cara is the sun, and anyone would feel lucky to be swept into her orbit. I'd gladly follow her every day for the rest of my life. If things were different, but they aren't. All she wants is something temporary.

I let go of her hip and take a step back.

"We can't."

Cara's eyes shoot up to mine, filled with hurt.

"Oh."

She gives me a small nod and takes a large step back toward my bedroom door.

"Right. Well, I'll just..." she stammers.

Cara looks toward the doorway and then back to me.

"I'll be downstairs."

"Cara. Wait. It's not because I don't want you."

"It's fine, Sinclair. We're partners. I got caught up in the moment. That's all. This is nothing."

Sting. Sting. Sting. Sting. Sting.

"Good. I'm glad we have that covered."

"See you in a few. We don't want to be late."

"We won't be."

Cara looks me up and down once more and then knocks on the bedroom door before leaving the room.

I sit down on my bed and take my head in my hands as it hangs.

"Just great." I sigh.

This isn't how I wanted this to go. I'm almost fifty years old; I can't let there be any miscommunication between the two of us. We're adults. Miscommunication is something grown adults just shouldn't let happen. Hell, she's in her mid-thirties, so I doubt she wants that either.

Tomorrow. After the mission tonight, I'll explain to her how crazed she's been making me and how it's my own feelings that I don't want to get in the way of what this is. I'm so fucking starved for love that I'm mistaking this time together as that.

Off my bed, I put the finishing touches on. My guns and knife. I know I'll be checked, but I don't go anywhere without them. Certainly not when I know I'm entering the lion's den.

Brad's warning was severe, but I'll take it for what he was saying. The Marlin is dangerous. We know this. The fact of the matter is my old friend is scared shitless. These are different times we're working in. It would be stupid of me not to take extra precautions with his warning.

Grabbing my cell phone, I head down the stairs to see Cara waiting by the front door, tapping away on her own phone.

"Everything okay?" I ask.

She looks up at me, almost panicked. Clearly, she's talking to someone about something she was wrapped up in.

"Everything's great. The car is here."

She grabs both sets of keys and tosses me one that I easily catch.

"Just in case we get separated."

"We won't," I counter.

"You never know."

Cara picks up her purse from the entryway table and opens the door. I quickly catch up and close it behind us before we descend the stairs to the black car.

"What did Brad say?" she asks as I open the car door.

"Nothing new."

"Figured." She slides into the backseat, then moves over to give me room to slide in after her.

"It was strange though," I offer as I shut the car door.

"Still heading to the Gem Casino?" the driver asks.

"Yes, please," Cara replies warmly.

"On our way. Should be less than a fifteen-minute drive."

"Thank you," she responds.

The driver raises the divider between us to give us privacy.

"What was so strange?" she asks me.

"He's scared beyond belief of the Marlin."

She tilts her head.

"Is that really a surprise?"

"No, but he's scared. Brad the Bull is fucking scared shitless."

"I see."

Cara takes one of my hands in hers.

"We'll help him through this. He doesn't have to go under for this."

"But he's culpable."

"We're after the Kingpin and the Marlin, not him."

"He said the Marlin's plans will be laid out here. Tonight is the biggest test for me, and then we're in."

"Then we'll be professional," she teases.

I smirk.

"Right. Professional. Lately, I'm beginning to wonder what the hell I've been doing being so professional my whole goddamn life."

Cara's hand tightens on mine. I didn't realize she had kept it there.

"We've got this, Grant. We do. Let's go in there and impress Cordelia. Snoop around. Find out what's next."

"You make it sound so simple."

"It's anything but simple," she starts before grinning.

"What?"

"But Mr. and Mrs. Weston are on the case."

She tilts her head to the side, and I can't help but laugh. Fuck, this woman gets all facets of me. Cara laughs freely, and it feels as though I'm peeling back the layers of the person I crave.

"That we are."

She did make me feel better.

"What did Ruby say?"

"Nothing new on her front. Said she would be in contact with Rob on your behalf and pass along any messages if need be."

"I'll have to check in with him too."

I pull out my cell phone and send him a quick text message, checking in and letting him know he can trust Ruby. If Cara and I are partners for now, then they need to be too.

TWELVE

Cara

HAVING to reassure Grant that we've got this was a nice position to be in. I always see him so stoic and domineering, almost as if he's been keeping his walls up more than I have when we're together.

I know part of him feels like he's the protector in our duo, but I can take care of myself. He knows that, but I think part of him does actually feel differently since we got married.

I understand that Brad's message came with a warning, yet so much was left unsaid. It was almost a plea to a friend to stay away and not get involved. If this were any other scenario, Brad's caution would be appreciated. It just fuels us even more, knowing how close we're getting to the action.

The relationship between Brad and Grant is clearly deeper than Grant told me. As much as I want his attention and eyes on me, I want him to let his guard down fully. I want his truths and explanations for the past. I want it all.

Pulling up to the casino, Grant escorts me out of the car and keeps my arm wrapped around his as he leads me up the double set of stairs. He tells a guard our names, who then verifies we're allowed to be here. All protocol is going as we assumed it would.

The guard tells us to go through the front door and take the elevator down to floor two. That's where the tournament will be starting soon.

As we get into the elevator, we're both quiet, not because of nervousness but because of all the planning and work that has led us here. We need to play our parts well and finally get into the inner circle of trust.

The elevator door dings and opens into a world of glitz, glamour, and guns. Too many guards with their firearms visible are walking along the perimeter of the floor.

People are laughing and drinking all around us. This isn't just for the seedy members who operate in the night; this is truly for the wealthy and elite to be part of as well.

"To the back. I see Brad."

I follow Grant's line of sight and see two guards stationed in front of another set of double doors. A group of people is waiting there, and one of them is Brad.

I spot Noelle nearby, with a glass of champagne in her hand, talking to a woman I haven't met yet. I assumed that could be the case. I'm going to have to play the role of the perfect wife here as I mingle with the other women.

This is possibly my biggest challenge. I grew up with boys and had very few girlfriends. As an adult, I've been so focused on work that I haven't made many female friends either. The only ones I truly know well are because of Lachlan, Grayson, and Liam.

I can make it happen. I've gotten to know women before.

"I see Noelle."

Grant spots her too.

"We're a team, Cara. All night. Okay?"

"Team Weston."

"Team Weston."

Cara laughs as we walk toward them.

"It's a little cheesy, you know?"

"I do, but it makes you smile, so I'll take it."

My breath hitches as I grip his arm tighter.

I'm getting my answers about Grant, one way or another.

Earlier tonight, I thought I was so close to him kissing me in private. Then words were mixed together, and I'm not sure why he didn't. It's as if I said something wrong, but I can't figure out what it was.

As we approach the group waiting to be let into the next room, Grant and I pull apart to go to the opposite sides. The sudden loss of his touch is overwhelming.

It's so hard to focus on what I should be, and I hate it. I'm not a woman who swoons over a man and lets him occupy her every thought. Yet there is so much behind what Grant knows and how he feels that I'm dying to discover.

"See you in there, love."

"Find me."

"Always."

He places a small kiss on my forehead, and my body melts into it. Grant steps away and starts to put on the façade of Ace Weston.

"Cara! You're here," Noelle shouts.

I close the distance to her and move farther away from Grant.

"Hi!"

We kiss each other on the cheek, and Noelle gestures to the unknown friend she was just speaking with.

"Aria, this is Cara Weston. Ace's wife."

Aria perks up.

"The one who captured the elusive Ace's heart. Well done," she says.

"Thank you," I answer, confused.

How does Aria know Ace?

"It's nice to meet you," I continue.

"You as well. You look so gorgeous, no wonder Ace was willing to come off the market for the looks of you," she says.

"Oh, Aria. Don't make Cara blush," Noelle says with a giggle.

"No, it's fine. How do you know Ace?"

"I don't, my dear. His reputation precedes him."

"Well, then, thank you for all the compliments. I know nothing of that sort about my Ace other than the way he eagerly tried to win my heart."

Aria looks annoyed but moves on easily.

I give her a half smile, and Noelle starts talking about the latest drama in the neighborhood. I learn that Aria isn't from around Charlotte but flew in for the event.

Ace and his reputation.

Another secret part of his past life that I have no idea about.

It's infuriating.

Maybe Cara Collins doesn't have a right to know about his past, but Cara Weston certainly does. This is more of what I can't make out about Grant.

Grant Sinclair is nothing but secrecy, deception, and lies. A trifecta I plan to unravel. He'll be at my mercy by the end of this.

As I stew on that interaction, I barely engage with the

conversation that Aria and Noelle are having. Maybe I do have to try harder to gain female friends, after all.

Aria steps away, and Noelle focuses her attention on me.

"Don't listen to Aria. Ace has never been anything but a gentleman."

"You know him well?"

"Not well, but..."

Commotion goes on behind us, catching our attention. It's the tournament doors opening and a sea of people entering.

"I know his character. That's all I need to know."

"How?"

"Ace saved Brad from a fire."

"I..." I stammer.

I compose myself as more noise erupts around us.

"I didn't know that. Thank you."

"I'm sure he's meant to tell you. It's a complicated past."

I smile, unsure if that's true.

"Let's go find our men before this starts."

Noelle loops her arm in mine and pulls me in their direction. At this rate, I'm beginning to feel like I'll be pulled at all night.

"HOW ARE YOU DOING, LOVE?" Grant asks.

I know it's all for show, but I can't help the way my heartbeat quickens every time he calls me that. Even when I'm so confused by who Grant really is.

"Okay. This is all something else. I've never been to a tournament at a casino before like this," I say.

"This one is over-the-top compared to others I've found myself in."

"With Brad in the time before?" I cock an eyebrow.

"Exactly," he says with furrowed eyes.

Chatter continues all around us, and it's growing louder by the minute since the last game ended.

"How do you think Cordelia is going to take me losing? I had to do it."

"I think she'll understand. I was watching your tricks, and I'm sure she could also tell what you were up to."

I revel in the warmth as he slips his arm around my back and places his hand on the lower part. We head toward the poker tournament table since blackjack just ended.

Grant finished second, much to everyone's surprise. As a newcomer, people were skeptical as to why he was able to play in said tournaments altogether. It wasn't until Cordelia shared that he was a special friend of hers that everyone closed their mouths.

Everyone is afraid of Cordelia Miller. Another sign of the power she holds, even outside of the fact that this is her casino.

"That's the only way I was going to get their trust for the rest of the night."

"It was the right move."

Grant and I approach the poker table. As we wait, he faces me completely.

"How did Cordelia look when I lost?"

"Like she understood. There was no sign of frustration or confusion. I promise. You don't have to second-guess yourself."

"Good. Then this is all going according to plan."

I look around the room and shake my head.

"What is it?"

"It's nothing," I say with a shrug of my shoulders.

"It's something."

"Mr. Weston, we're ready for you to take your seat," a host interjects.

Grant gives him a curt nod before focusing back on me.

"Come with me."

He takes a seat in his assigned chair and pulls me into the open seat next to him. The other players are still gathering, and it doesn't look to be an issue for anyone just yet.

"Grant, I have to get up."

He leans forward, and I want to hold onto the look in his eyes forever.

"I need to know what you were thinking."

"One of these days..." I say as I lean back slightly and hang my arm on the back of the chair.

"What?" he asks with a twinkle in his eyes and a lopsided smile.

"One of these days, you'll have to tell me all your lies."

Grant gets serious, and he nods, almost to himself. He flashes me a wide smile and adjusts his jacket. When I start to stand, he gently catches one of my arms. Looking down at him, I wait for what he needs to say.

"Stay close. You're my lucky charm, remember?"

I roll my eyes playfully as I swat his shoulder.

"How could I forget? All those years of calling me your lucky charm, and now, here we are."

"Who would have guessed it?"

"Certainly not me," I tease.

"Believe me, I know. What is it you said?"

Grant feigns confusion before a teasing smile takes over his expression.

"You'll never be my anything."

"Looks like you won that battle."

Heat simmers in Grant's eyes, and I know there is so much we need to talk about between us. This isn't the right time.

"For now."

I swallow thickly as the announcer starts talking. Grant puts on his sunglasses and lets go of our embrace.

"Stay close."

"I will."

I take a few steps back to leave him to the game. Suddenly, a figure stands beside me.

"He'll win."

I look over my shoulder to see it's none other than Cordelia.

"He will."

"Confident. I like that."

"He has more than skills."

She chuckles softly.

"I knew I had a good feeling about you both. Ace's past speaks for him. You, on the other hand, I wasn't too sure about until I did a little check."

"You ran a background check on me?"

"I asked around."

Our eyes meet.

"And you passed, sweetheart," she finishes.

Without another word, Cordelia focuses on the first round that's getting underway. I do the same, knowing that all the steps we took actually worked.

Ace and Cara Weston are in as long as Grant can pass the final test and win this tournament.

The dealer starts the first round, and I focus on Grant. The way his demeanor completely changes when he's in the game is alarming. It shouldn't be, but all of this makes me wonder how much more there is to Grant Sinclair.

I want all his secrets for my own.

There are ten players at the table with a minimum buy-in of a thousand dollars for this first round. I can't imagine where we'll go from here.

As I scan the other players, I notice they are all wearing glasses or some type of facial coverings to try and hide their expressions.

I pause at one person who is wearing a black ball cap and no glasses—our neighbor Fred, whom we met at the barbecue. I chew on my lower lip, trying to remember his file.

Fred Jones. Single. No children. Living out in the suburbs of North Carolina. He's involved somehow with all of this; I'm just not sure how yet.

Maybe if Grant wins, we'll find out more of the intimate details of everyone's roles.

He glances up at me and then focuses back on his cards.

What is a single man doing living in the middle of the suburbs like this? I'm not saying someone like him can't, but given the neighborhood and the fact he's here tonight, it just feels suspicious. Now that I think of it, Grant and I haven't dived too far into his background outside of the norm.

Maybe we should if he's one of the ten at the table.

"Here you go," Noelle whispers as she hands me a glass of champagne.

"Thank you," I murmur.

She stands next to me so that I'm now wedged between her and Cordelia, who is flanked by her personal bodyguards.

One by one, players are being eliminated, and apparently, they aren't allowed to buy back in. Once you're out, you're out.

Remaining at the table are Grant, Fred, and two people

I have yet to formally meet—a woman named Taby and a man called Rick.

Taby looks at me intensely as the next round of cards is dealt.

I have seen Taby around in the neighborhood, but nothing out of the norm. She must be involved in this somehow too. Grant and I have to investigate our neighbors further.

Another round takes place, and Fred is eliminated.

The anger spiraling behind his eyes is off-putting and makes me question what exactly he had riding on this tournament outside of the winning pot.

Looking over at Cordelia, I see a twitch in her jaw. Perhaps he was being tested too.

Thinking back, Fred Jones moved into the neighborhood not long before Grant and I did. Months maybe. It's not like everyone who lives in the neighborhood is part of this ring. Some people are truly innocent, yet I have a feeling Fred isn't. He must be like us, trying to get involved for some reason.

His file didn't bring back any known arrests. He's white collar, running several interconnected businesses. Maybe he's trying to use the Carolinas mafia to get a piece of the pie.

The rounds continue until it's finally just Grant and Taby left in the tournament. A sly grin stretches across Taby's face as soon as she gets her cards. I wish I could see Grant's expression better.

The tension in the air is thick, and it feels as though this round is taking hours instead of mere minutes.

Noelle places a gentle hand on my shoulder, and I realize that I've been frozen in place, methodically watching each move. Cordelia shifts her weight, and I realize that she's more invested than I am in seeing who wins.

Other card games are happening after this, but something tells me the poker tournament is the one to watch.

Grant raises Taby and places what could be the final bet.

Taby eyes her cards carefully, and for the first time all night, I sense uncertainty there.

Sucking in a deep breath of air, I wait, like everyone around me, to see what her move will be. Is this woman going to be the one to stop Grant?

Taby smiles widely and lays out her cards. Grant follows suit, and I slowly see a winning hand flash before me.

He did it. Grant beat Taby and won the poker tournament.

Cordelia starts to clap next to me, and soon, sounds erupt from around the room. Grant and Taby get up from their seats and shake hands. She says something to him, and he gives her a small nod before pulling away.

Grant's eyes search the audience until they land on mine.

He flashes me a breathtaking smile, one that makes my skin prick with goose bumps.

This man of mine won. We're in. After tonight, it should be smooth sailing, and I can finally make the real move I've been wanting to make on my husband.

Grant steps through the crowd of well-wishers until he finally reaches me.

"What do you think, Mrs. Weston?"

I wrap my arms around his neck and stare up at him.

"You did good, Mr. Weston."

I bite down on my lip in indecision.

"Cara," he whispers as he lowers his head and rests his forehead on mine.

"Hmm?"

"We shouldn't."

"We should."

"I'm too old for you."

"You're perfect."

"I'm too set in my ways."

"I don't care."

"What about your dad?"

"He loves you."

"What about everything else?"

"We'll talk about it."

Our breaths grow shallow, and I know what I want him to do.

"Fuck it."

I grin.

"Can I kiss you?" he rasps.

"Yes."

Grant pulls back, and we're once again staring at each other with something ablaze in our eyes.

This is it—it's real. He feels it, too, no matter how wrong or right it might be.

He bends down and places a kiss on my lips. It's warm and soft, everything I remembered it to be. I try to deepen it, and a stifled groan comes out of Grant's mouth.

I nibble on his lower lip before requesting access to go deeper.

"Fuck," he murmurs.

Next thing I know, his hand is on the back of my head, gripping a pile of my hair tightly as he kisses me like I've never been kissed before. My body is on fire from just this kiss, and I know that he's everything I want and more.

Out of breath, he pulls back and rests his slightly damp forehead against mine. Our breaths are ragged as we both process what just transpired between us.

"That was…" I whisper.

"Everything."

We stay in this position until the clack of loud heels approaches. We break apart, but Grant keeps one hand on my waist as he pulls me into his side.

Cordelia and Taby.

"Well, that was something else," Cordelia says.

"The kiss or the way the man played?" Taby asks slyly.

I pretend to blush into Grant's shoulder like any ordinary wife would. Instead, I'm consumed by an unfamiliar possessiveness, and it takes everything inside me to remember that I'm a professional and our plans are working.

I can't tell if Taby is interested in Grant for something other than cards. Jealousy comes through, and I have to smile to prevent saying something I'll regret and ruin what advancements we've made.

"Thank you," he answers.

"Sit out the next rounds. Wait in that room," Taby starts as she gestures to a guarded door behind where they are.

"And we'll be in when this ends."

"What's in there?" Grant asks.

"Your future," Taby answers.

My eyes flash to Cordelia's, and I realize that we got it all wrong.

Cordelia isn't the Kingpin—it's Taby.

THIRTEEN

Grant

I TAKE Cara's hand tightly in mine as we make our way through the boisterous crowd of gamblers and spectators to the back room.

Originally, I was under the impression that I would have to continue to compete all night to prove my worth, but it was clearly displayed during the two I played.

As I took Cara's hand in mine, the flicker of realization dawned on me. Taby has been the main player this whole time. Cordelia works for her and has the over-the-top guards to distract from the truth.

What we've already uncovered here is beyond what we would have been able to without being in the field and ingrained with this crew.

Cara squeezes my hand as we approach the guarded door. She looks straight ahead, trying not to cause any potential issues. It's hard to focus on anything now that I have her.

Is catching the Kingpin and the Marlin really worth the idea of losing her? I know she's strong and capable, but I can't let anything happen to this woman. Not when it seems like we are finally on the same page.

Earlier, she asked me if I could tell her all my lies, and I understood what wasn't said. Cara and I have big conversations we need to have. It's not just my lies but her truths that need to be told out loud.

When she asked me that, I knew at that moment that I was going to make her mine forever. Cara may be my wife on paper, but I want it to be real.

I'm done playing pretend with Cara.

How could I deny her when she clearly wanted more? That kiss was palpable, and it solidified things between us. We've come so far, and after this mission, I want to make her my wife in every sense of the word forever.

"Taby asked us to wait in here," I say to a guard.

"You're on the list..." His eyebrows shoot up in surprise.

"Is everything okay?"

"Permanently," he finishes.

Wow, that's a shock to us as well.

The guard opens the door and lets us walk through.

Inside the room feels like another world—a darker one where I recognize so many people from the neighborhood and from all our preparations.

We take our seats on a set of empty barstools at the sleek all-black bar and settle in, trying to pretend this isn't what we've been dying for.

There could be any number of cameras in this room, so Cara and I will have to talk to one another in code to confirm the plan is a go.

"I think Taby will want to speak to me privately," I say.

"Of course."

A bartender approaches us, and I order a whiskey neat, and Cara orders a glass of champagne.

"I'll be here," she says as she looks around the room.

I watch as something catches her eye—a door with a code panel next to it. That has to be the Kingpin's office.

"Maybe I'll get into a bit of mischief with one of these gentlemen," she pretends to tease.

The bartender gives us our drinks.

We take them and give each other a slight cheers.

"Don't get into too much trouble without me, love."

"I wouldn't dare."

She sips her champagne, and a playful expression takes over.

"Although I have a feeling that's unavoidable."

Right.

No doubt, there will be some type of security system outside the door panel to access the Kingpin's office.

"Maybe I'll join in on the fun if I can break away."

"You'll have to come find me."

"Mr. Weston?" a soft voice asks.

Cara and I both turn around to find a petite woman with a clipboard in hand.

"Please come with me."

"Can my wife come?" I ask.

The woman smiles warmly as she glances between us both.

"No."

She turns around and starts walking away, expecting me to follow.

"Duty calls," I whisper to Cara.

"See you soon."

I catch up to the woman in question and am led through the very security door that we were just eyeing. The woman enters a passcode that I know Cara will catch, allowing her to enter moments after we go through.

"Where are we headed?" I ask casually.

"To Ms. Turner's private quarters. They're waiting for you."

"Private quarters?"

"She doesn't do this kind of business in the office."

"Fair enough."

Interesting. That means we'll have to come back tonight and break into these private quarters. Cara may find something in the office, but no doubt, there is something in here that's important.

Walking through the door, we head down a dark, long hallway. As we weave in and out, I'm discovering this is much larger than Cara or I assumed it would be.

The woman pauses before we go down another hallway. She enters another code on a discreet side panel.

I try to get the code, but it's entered quickly and away from my line of sight. What does that look like? Four, nine, two, zero? I'll have to share the pattern right away with Cara when I see her next.

Suddenly, bright lights turn on one by one, illuminating the hallway.

"Right through there, they're waiting for you," she says with her arm extended.

"By myself?"

"Yes."

The woman leaves my side and walks back the way we just came.

I adjust the cuffs of my jacket and head toward Taby and Cordelia.

Step by step, I take in my surroundings. It's interesting, really. There are high-security details and a hallway that no one would be the wiser of unless they had been taken down here before, like I am right now.

It would have taken us a while to discover this wing and its significance.

I pause at the door.

I could be walking into a trap instead of being offered some type of deal. There's also the possibility that they've discovered I'm really a spy in their midst.

Nothing about this is normal.

I reach for the handle and pull it down.

Well, looks like I'm about to find out.

THE ROOM I walk into is lavish, with crystal chandeliers and red leather everywhere I look—from the seating to the walls, and it's over-the-top—probably Taby's preference.

"Welcome," a sultry voice greets me.

Taby.

She's at the bar, pouring a drink.

"Would you like one?" she asks without turning around.

"I'd love one."

I walk over to where she stands and see Cordelia sitting in a nearby room, not paying attention to us.

Taby pours two whiskeys neat into crystal glasses.

"I like what you've done here."

She faces me with her ruby-red lips and a suggestive expression. I take in what she's wearing for the first time: a black, tight-fitting dress that exposes her long legs and fake breasts.

Taby extends a glass to me.

"Thank you."

She grins and gives a slight shake of her head.

"Follow me."

She leads us over to a red leather circular sofa, and I sit on the side opposite her.

"What am I doing here?" I ask.

"Patience must not be something you possess."

She takes a sip of her drink as she crosses one leg over the other. I lean back in my seat and wait for her to continue. It's clear that Taby is trying to lure me into her fold. The art of seduction must be one of her usual ploys with men like me.

"Oh, you're no fun, I see."

"I can be from time to time."

She leans forward, and her breasts start to spill over the edge of her dress.

"How fun?" she asks.

Ordinarily, I would give in to what she's asking for. A beautiful woman in a position of power, whom I need something from.

Only things are different now. I haven't even started with Cara, so I can't mess it up, even if it is part of the job.

"I'm a married man," I say while showing her my ring.

She grins and then laughs wildly as she sits back.

"Rare."

With a bob of her head, she takes another sip of her whiskey.

"Good."

I swallow down my whiskey and set the glass on the table.

"I have a job for you."

"I'm listening."

"In two days. On the coast. Go to this address at this time," she says as she slides a paper across the table.

"There's a poker tournament being hosted by one of my

colleagues. Win. The prize is in diamonds. My contact needs you to win in order for the deal to be made."

"Why?"

"Don't go asking questions you don't want the answers to."

"What if I do?"

She considers this.

"Win the tournament and then come back here. I'll let you know more if you can deliver the diamonds."

"I take it these are special."

"To say the least."

I glance to my side and see Cordelia still in the other room, paying us no attention.

"Can I ask you a question?"

Taby shrugs as she tucks her legs underneath her and kicks her heels off one by one.

"Who are you?"

She laughs, reaching an arm behind her on the couch.

"Baby, if you don't know by now, then you aren't as smart as I thought you were."

"The Kingpin."

"Such an odd term for a woman in power, wouldn't you say? No matter, I fought for my place here. One kill and deal at a time."

Got her. She's admitted that she's the Kingpin of Charlotte and is sharing so casually about how she came to be.

"Does that scare you?" she asks.

"No."

"Good. It would be terribly boring if it did."

I pause, unsure of what she expects from me.

"You're something different, Ace. I can tell. That doesn't mean you're going to pan out for what we need, but time will tell."

"I'll do whatever it takes."

"Not whatever it takes. You've just proven that."

When I turned her down, anger had flashed across her face.

"You can go now," she says with a fling of her hand. She gulps down the remainder of the whiskey and gets up with the glass in hand.

"Now," she calls out as she saunters over to the bar.

Getting off the couch, I head to the door without another word.

I walk through the winding hallway and find myself back at the crossroads with the main door entrance to my left and what has to be the hallway to the office to the right.

If anyone finds me, I'll just claim I'm lost.

I take a right and easily find Taby's office. Her assistant is nowhere to be found as I walk past a desk and open the main office door.

It's dark inside, so I pull out a flashlight from my pocket. After turning it on, I shine it around the room and still.

"Cara?" I whisper to the figure.

"It's me," she says, almost out of breath.

"Let's get out of here."

"I need to search one more spot."

"It's pointless. I'll explain when we leave."

Cara steps out of the darkness with a perplexed look.

"What happened?"

"I found her quarters. We'll have to come back."

"Private quarters? At the casino?"

Cara searches my expression for any sign of what happened.

"I promise. I'll tell you at home."

"Okay. I trust you."

Fuck, that's good to hear.

BACK HOME, Cara and I silently go into our separate rooms. I take a quick shower and change into a pair of black joggers and a white T-shirt, something casual after the long night we've had.

We're so close to catching the Marlin, I can taste it. The only problem is I need Taby to introduce me. If I take on these small missions for her, then hopefully, I'll gain her trust, and she'll tell me the truth.

As I leave my room, Cara comes out of hers at the same time.

She looks breathtaking in a silky pair of pajamas that I don't think she would normally wear around me. The tiny shorts have a hint of lace trim to them that also outlines the top of the matching low-cut tank.

Cara's chest heaves as she watches me drink her in.

"Beautiful," I say.

"Come on, lover boy," she teases as she takes my hand in hers and leads me down the stairs.

I'll gladly follow this woman anywhere.

Tonight, we admitted the first of our truths to one another. I know I have a lot more to share with her, and this is it.

"Want a drink? Water? Wine? Vodka?" I say to lighten the mood.

Cara takes my wrist in between her delicate hands and pulls the face of my watch in her direction.

"It's three a.m."

"Wine it is," I rasp.

She smiles as she lets go of my hand.

"I'll get the glasses out if you can find a bottle."

She bends down and pulls out two glasses from a bar

cabinet. I open the wine fridge and find a vintage bottle of a cabernet.

Another comfortable silence lingers as she slides the glasses over to me and I pour the wine. She takes hers, and I do the same.

Walking over to the living room, Cara slides onto one side of the sofa and pats the seat cushion for me to join her.

As I sit down, I notice a hint of something new in Cara's expression.

"Is everything okay?" I ask.

"Did she come on to you?"

Cara's eyes are on mine as she waits.

"Yes."

Cara nods and takes a large gulp of her drink.

"I told her no," I continue.

Her eyes snap up to mine as she lowers the glass.

"You know you shouldn't have."

"Yes, I should have."

Cara sighs and settles further into the pillows behind her.

"Grant, I would have understood."

"I wouldn't have," I counter.

"You wouldn't have?"

"No. It's different now. Don't you agree?"

Cara's breath hitches at the declaration.

"I suppose I do."

She leans forward and sets her wine down. I take a sip of mine and set it down on the coffee table as well.

She comes closer to where I am and fidgets with her hands in her lap.

"We need to talk," I say.

"Yes. Yes, we do. Grant..."

"Let me go first."

"Okay," she says, relieved.

"Since the day I met you, I have always known that something was different about you. From the way you handled yourself to the fierce look of determination you would get when I challenged you, I always knew that you were different."

Cara laughs lightly.

"I hope this is a good thing."

"Love, it's the best thing."

She swallows and focuses on me.

"You call me that now."

"I do."

"I thought it was something just in the field. Something pretend."

"It's not. Do you really think I've been pretending this whole time?"

"No, I don't."

"Can you say the same?"

"Are you asking if I've been pretending?"

"Yes, I am."

"No, I haven't been since the day we said 'I do.'"

"Me either." A faint blush stains her cheeks.

"What about the other day?"

"What do you mean?"

"You said you wanted this to be temporary."

She looks confused.

"Ahead of the casino?"

I nod.

"I was scared. Afraid that you would only want me for the time being, so I was trying to say what I thought you wanted to hear. I'd been driving myself crazy trying to get your attention. I normally don't have to work that hard," she admits.

"I've wanted you since that very first time I saw you."

She gasps and tries to regroup. The hem of her shirt rises, revealing a sliver of her tight stomach.

"So distracting." I grip the end of it and pull it down slightly.

"Come on, it's just a little skin."

"You can walk around naked, but right now, I'm trying not to kiss you."

She moves closer to me and takes my hands in hers.

"I know we have a lot to discuss. A lot of the past that you need answers to. But being with you out here. Getting married. Going through this together. Finding a true partner in you. It's done something to me."

"What has it done?"

"You know."

"Tell me."

"It's made me fall in love with you."

FOURTEEN

Cara

MY HEART IS BEATING WILDLY at Grant's confession.

Love.

It's what I've been feeling as well through all the small touches and stolen glances, but I didn't think it was being reciprocated. I've never truly been in love before, but every word that Grant is saying resonates with me.

"I love you," I confess.

Grant hangs his head back, and a relieving breath of air rushes out.

"I love you, *my love.*"

Without another thought about the past or future, all I can focus on is the present.

I wrap my arms around his neck and place a gentle kiss on his lips. Grant groans and pushes my head forward to deepen it. His tongue demands entry, which I gladly give him.

This isn't calculated or cautious like our previous kisses;

this is a declaration of love between us. So much that we've both wanted to say is coming out in this moment.

His hands roam the length of my back before settling on my ass. He grips my cheeks roughly and forces me into his lap. My knees go outside each of his legs as he begins to grind me against his hard length.

"Oh!" I yelp.

He chuckles before finding my mouth again and kissing me roughly. My hands go to his hair as I pull harshly with each thrust against his crotch.

I lean away from him and let my head hang back. My long hair is teasing his legs as he drags me continuously against his length. My eyes shut as I feel ecstasy bubbling inside.

Warmth fills every inch of my body as if it's never been this ablaze before. I knew Grant would be able to play my body easily after the few times we've touched, but I never expected it to feel like this.

My heart belongs to Grant, and now so will my body.

"Fuck," I moan as I grip tightly onto his shoulders.

"That's it, love. Make a mess on me."

"Grant," I whimper.

It just encourages him to go faster as he senses I'm close to coming.

Wetness fills my silky shorts, and I should have known that these were a bad choice.

"Look at you, chasing your pleasure. It's a sight to behold."

I start to grind my sex against his hard cock and know that any second, I'm going to come for the first time by this man who has become my undoing.

"That's it. Give it to me. Let me watch you come for the first time."

"Fuck, fuck, fuck," I scream as my nails dig into his shoulders, and I still on top of him. He moves away from my ass and grips my hips to encourage me to keep going.

Light bursts from within as I come harder than I thought was possible.

As it fades away, Grant stops pulling me against his cock as I catch my breath. With my eyes still shut tight, I can't believe that I just came without his cock even being inside me. It only took minutes; I don't even know if I've ever made myself come that quickly before.

I feel a light sheen of sweat gathering on my face and pieces of my hair clinging to my skin.

"Perfection. Utter perfection getting to see you come," he rasps.

My eyes snap open to find Grant's fiery gaze on me.

"I've..." I start.

I giggle in disbelief.

"I don't want to give you a bigger ego than you already have," I tease.

"Oh please, love. Tell me."

I rest my forehead on his and feel his sweat too. As I try to come down from my high, I want to say it. Adjusting on top of him, I feel his hard cock underneath me. I pull back and smile.

"Tell me, love," he says with a grin.

"I've never come that hard before in my life, and you weren't even inside me."

That grin widens.

"See," I say as I swat his shoulder playfully.

"I fucking love that."

"Of course you do."

"Not even by yourself?"

"I'm not even going to entertain your question. I just told you the truth."

"Well, I'm not against an assist with a toy, but I think I'll get you even further than this."

All the teasing is gone as we both focus on his growing erection. I widen my legs slightly to let it settle between my folds and start rocking my hips. The way he thickens with each small thrust only makes me wetter.

"You want this cock inside you?"

"Yes," I whimper.

"Come on, love."

Grant hoists me up to stand on the floor, keeping his hands on me the whole time as he gets up next to me.

A wide smile stretches across his face as he bends and scoops me up.

I yelp as I cling to him, and my arms naturally go around his neck.

"What are you doing?" I say with a light laugh.

"Bedding my bride."

"You would have carried me to bed if we were married for real?" I ask as he walks.

Grant pauses at the foot of the stairs.

"We were married *for real*. Nothing about this is fake to me."

"I thought it was just a convenience."

He laughs.

"Love, I mean this in the best way possible, but nothing about this is convenient."

I shrug slightly as I hold onto him.

Grant easily takes the stairs two at a time.

"My room?" I ask.

"Fine by me."

He kicks my slightly ajar door open and stalks into my bedroom, then gently places me on the bed.

"I didn't take you to be like this," I say.

"What'd you expect? For me to treat the love of my life like an animal?"

"Maybe I want the animalistic side of you."

Grant laughs darkly.

"Believe me, you'll be seeing every side of me. You drive me absolutely crazy."

I whimper at the idea.

"I love that."

I move to the center of the bed and lean back on my arms. Grant keeps his eyes on me as he walks around to the front of the bed.

"Look at you. Beautiful as the best dream and all mine."

"All yours."

Fire blazes in his eyes as he leans forward and rests his hands on the edge of the bed.

"You know that's what you are."

"It's all I want to be."

"Come here," he whispers.

I get up onto all fours and slowly crawl along the length of the bed.

"Look at you, being my fantasy come to life. Coming to me the way I requested. You're dangerous like I've always desired," he says.

"What are you going to do with me then?"

I sit back and let my legs dangle between his arms.

"Lie back, love. I need another."

I tilt my head to the side in confusion.

"Lie back. Let me take care of you."

"Me?"

"Yeah, you're the only one in the room with me," he taunts.

"What about you?"

"Don't worry about me. Now let me get a taste. I've been dying to find out what you taste like."

"You have?"

Grant grins.

"Collins. Get your back on the bed now. The only words you're allowed to say next are fuck, please, or yes, sir."

I grin.

"Yes, sir."

I fall against the bed, and my hair spills all around me. Grant's hands go to the waistband of my shorts, and he slowly pulls them off. The silk teases my skin as he takes his time pulling them past my hips, down my thighs, and finally along the length of my shins and feet.

I feel the light weight of them gone altogether.

"No panties," he gruffly says, almost to himself.

"No. I knew what I wanted when I changed."

"Fucking perfection."

Grant dips low and pulls my hips forward so I'm slightly off the bed. He takes my legs and puts them on his shoulders.

He dips his head between my legs, and I'm instantly soaking wet from his proximity. Grant inhales deeply, and it's the most aroused I've ever felt in my life. I've had one life-changing sexual experience with this man in less than an hour, and that's far more than I've ever had in my over thirty years of life.

Grant's palm starts to caress my sex, and moments later, his tongue is licking up my seam. My hands shoot up above my head, and I try to grasp onto anything.

"Fuck," I whimper.

Grant starts licking more powerfully as if I'm the best thing he's ever tasted. It's overwhelming how much I can't take yet need all at once.

"Oh my god," I scream right as his palm finds the exact spot.

My legs squeeze around his head, and my hands shoot up to grip his hair.

"Don't stop, please. Don't stop."

"Never."

I feel a hint of a laugh as Grant continues hitting the right spot. As soon as I'm about to come, his tongue hits me just right, and I explode.

"Grant," I scream into the abyss.

My arms fall to my side, and my legs widen as they fall limp.

Grant grips my thighs as he stands.

"I'll never get over the sound of you calling out my name."

I laugh as he's just delivered my second orgasm of the night, and he's the one standing in awe of me.

"I..." I start.

"Hush, love. That was just the beginning."

I peer forward as Grant slides off his joggers. Just looking at his thick, muscular thighs makes me wet all over again.

He chuckles as he lifts his white T-shirt over his head, and my heart flutters.

I feel like I'm watching a personalized porn video made just for me. His chest is perfection, with rippling abs and defined pecs that I can't help but stare at.

"Love, if you keep looking at me like that, I might come in my boxers," he jokes.

"I wouldn't mind."

"I'd like to feel you wrapped around my cock. I'm sure that'll happen eventually if you keep prancing around the house like you have been."

I bite my lip to stifle a moan as I nod my head vigorously.

"Now that that's settled, why don't you take off that excuse for a tank top?"

I look down and realize that my silky sleep top is practically transparent, and my nipples are poking through.

"Whoops," I say with a giggle.

Sitting upright, I take off the tank top and toss it to the ground.

"Better?"

"Love, your tits are the best fucking pair on the planet."

I blush into my shoulder.

"Don't go getting bashful on me."

"Never," I answer as I lie back down.

Grant pulls off his tight boxer briefs, and his long, thick cock springs free.

My eyes widen momentarily.

"Don't worry, it'll fit."

"I hope so."

Grant climbs onto the bed, and I can't peel my eyes away from his cock. It's weeping from the tip, and for some reason, all I can think about is having his cum fill me up.

"I can't get you pregnant on a mission," he says, almost reading my mind.

"I'm on the pill, anyway."

Grant grips his cock in his hand, and my wetness pools even more. I'm a dripping mess on my bed just from watching him touch himself.

"I know you trust me, but I'm clean."

"I figured, given our line of work. I am too."

Grant continues to grip his cock as he kneels before me. I widen my legs as I brace for him to enter.

"A pink, pretty pussy all glistening just for me."

"Just for you."

He lines his cock up with my entrance and starts teasing the tip of it along my slit. It's erotic and sensual and damn frustrating because I want him to stop teasing me.

I whimper as I thrust forward, trying to get him inside.

"Patience, my love."

My heart soars at the nickname that I know is true. I'll never tire of hearing him call me that.

Grant stops and slowly pushes in. His thickness is almost too much to bear, but I want him to continue.

I claw at his back as my hands search eagerly for any part of him to hold onto as he keeps inching forward.

"Almost there," he murmurs.

"Yes," I groan.

Grant thrusts into me one final time, and I know he's completely in.

"I feel so full," I whimper.

"Don't worry, you'll adjust."

He pauses for a moment to give me a chance to settle into this sensation.

"Grant."

"Yes, love?"

"I need you to fuck me now."

He chuckles as he picks up one of my legs to get deeper inside me.

"With pleasure."

He thrusts, and it's the best kind of pain I could ask for. Grant knows my body so well, and it's only the first time we've been intimate.

As he continues to thrust and grind his hips deeper, I know I'm about to come for a third time already.

"Wait, I don't want to come yet."

Grant shakes his head briefly.

"I'm going to have you coming all morning."

"Fuck," I moan.

Another thrust, and the same fiery sensation starts building inside again.

"I'm about to come," I practically shout.

"Good," he says with another deep thrust.

My nails dig deep into his shoulder as my breasts bounce wildly from his movements.

"Your pussy is so tight. I can feel it contracting around my cock, begging for relief."

"Then keep going." I groan.

Grant wraps my leg around his waist and lets go of it. With his newly adjusted position, he palms my clit once again, and that sends me over.

"Scream for your husband, wife."

And I do.

Over and over again until I'm limp, lying in bed next to my husband, whom I love.

FIFTEEN

Grant

WITH THE WOMAN of my dreams in my hold, I can't imagine life getting any better than this. We have a lot to work through, but I never thought I'd find someone who would be my true counterpart in life.

Cara stirs in my arms, and I still. After a long, eventful night, we didn't get to bed until the sun was rising.

We have a busy night ahead of us, but for now, I'll live in this moment. There's plenty of time to worry about the mission, Luke's reaction, and the conversations that we need to have.

"Go back to sleep," Cara mumbles against my chest.

I try to stifle my laughter.

"Ugh," she groans.

"Not a morning person. Noted."

She rubs her hand against my chest, and it stirs my cock to life.

"Coffee?" I ask.

Her hand travels down the length of my chest and stomach until she finally reaches the waistband of my boxers.

Slowly, her hand gropes the outline of my cock.

"What are you thinking?" I groan.

Cara starts to rub it back and forth until I'm firmly hard and in her hold.

"I'm thinking I can't get enough of you," she murmurs.

With her still snuggled into my side, I use my other hand to travel beneath her shirt, caressing her as I go. I reach my destination of her perfect handful of breasts.

She whimpers as I start to massage them.

Cara removes her hand from the top of my boxers and dips it beneath the waistband. Her warm hand wraps around my cock, and it starts leaking onto her fingertips.

"Such a perfect girl," I say as she grips my cock and moves methodically back and forth.

"You're so big. I can't believe this was inside of me."

"I'd like to be again."

"Mmm, but isn't this nice?"

"That's putting it mildly."

I tweak one of her nipples, and she moans into my ear.

That's it.

I remove my hand from underneath her shirt and Cara's from inside my boxers.

"What?" she asks, confused.

In one swift motion, I grip her waist and pull her on top of me. She yelps in surprise as she tries to find her balance.

I lift the hem of her shirt, taking it off and throwing it onto the ground. She goes back to balancing her hands on my chest. It gives me the opportunity to lean slightly forward and pull down my boxers. I kick them off, and they roll up into the sheets.

"That was slick," she says with a giggle.

I grin as I lift her up slightly and position her bare pussy over my cock.

"You're drenched."

"It's what you seem to do to me."

She keeps a hold on my chest as she starts to grind against the length of my cock.

"I need to be inside you immediately."

I grip her hips and pop her up slightly to line up my erect cock. She helps me as she slowly slides onto it.

"Fuck," she moans with her head hanging back.

"That's it," I say to encourage her.

Fully on my cock, she adjusts to the position. The vision of her rocking slowly and her tits bouncing is incredible.

"I love the way you look riding me."

Cara opens her eyes and peers down. She starts to rock harder, and it makes her tits look like she's a porn star fucking me as a show.

I fold my arms beneath my head.

"Use me. This cock is for your pleasure."

She starts to ride me harder and lets out little whimpers as she goes.

"Grant," she moans as she goes faster.

I can tell my girl is getting close from the way she shuts her eyes and gets lost in chasing her pleasure.

"I'm going to come inside you."

"Yes," she whimpers.

That sets her off, and she starts to scream.

My girl's a screamer, and I fucking love it. I follow behind her and let my cum seep into her pussy.

Out of breath, Cara makes eye contact with me once again, and I can't help but let a smug smile stretch across my face.

Making this woman come is going to be my lifelong goal.

"Well, good morning," Cara teases.

"A very good morning for me."

She blushes and then starts to get off my cock. I instantly feel the loss.

As she heads into her bathroom, I love seeing her body sway as she goes. She looks over her shoulder at me as if she knew I was watching her.

"I'm never going to take my eyes off you again."

"Good. I like you a little possessive."

She disappears from my line of sight. Possessive? This woman is my wife. That doesn't even begin to describe how I feel about keeping her safe and mine.

I hop out of bed, find my discarded boxers, and put them on first, followed by my same joggers and shirt from last night.

As I finish getting dressed, a naked Cara comes out of the bathroom.

"I'll start some coffee."

"That'd be great. I'll meet you down there. I have to check in with Ruby again."

"Maybe I need a new assistant because Rob isn't as forthcoming as he usually is."

"He's just holding down your whole office. Cut him some slack."

"You're right."

I step forward and place a gentle kiss on top of her head as I wrap her in my arms. She brings her arms around me, and I love the feel of her bare tits pressed against me.

"I'm going to want to fuck you again if we keep at this," I tease.

"I wouldn't object."

I groan, and it makes Cara laugh.

"I'll see you down there," I say and place another kiss on top of her head.

"THAT SMELLS GREAT," Cara says as she walks into the living room.

The news is on low in the background, and I've opened the curtains to let the natural light in. Cara's in a fitted tank top and yoga pants.

She picks up her coffee and gets settled, curled up at my side. I wrap my arm around her and start to rub her arm.

"This is nice," she says.

Cara takes a sip of her coffee and then glances up at me. Indecision fills her expression.

"You know how I like my coffee?" she asks.

"We've been living together for a while. It's an easy thing to learn."

"Not for everyone."

"Catching on to how you like your coffee is the bare minimum, love."

Cara smiles shyly before focusing back on the news.

"I have a question for you," I say.

"What's that?"

"Why didn't you meet me in Willow Park that night?"

"The night we discovered one another?"

"Yes."

Cara moves up and shifts on the couch to face me. She grips her coffee mug.

"I couldn't believe it was you."

"That I know."

"I didn't know what to say."

"We could have started off differently."

"I was afraid. This job is something that is mine. At the time, I was so young and unsure of my direction. This job made me who I am, and I didn't want to share it with anyone in the real world."

"Which would have been me."

"Yes. You're such good friends with my parents, and even though I knew you wouldn't tell them, it just felt like this special thing I had for myself was going to be taken away. So I just decided to pretend like it didn't happen."

"Until we kept running into each other."

She smiles, but then it turns down.

"Yeah."

"What's wrong?"

"I wish I had handled it differently."

"Well, I don't think either of us assumed this would happen between us."

"No, I suppose not."

She takes a sip of her coffee, and I set mine down on the coffee table.

"Can I ask you something?" she asks.

"Of course."

"Did you really not remember what happened in Barcelona when you took the Holden contract?"

Barcelona.

Fuck.

I hadn't at the time, but now, as I watch the love of my life look pained, I remember it all. What she told me about them not believing in her as a woman, not feeling good enough in the field, all of it.

"You didn't," she whispers, relieved.

"Cara, I promise I didn't. I wouldn't have done business with them at all if I had. Do you believe me?"

She sets down her coffee and then takes my hands in hers.

"I do."

"Fuck. I feel terrible."

"Don't. Really. I believe you."

"I'm sorry."

"Thank you," she says with a squeeze of my hands.

"Do you remember what you said to me that night?"

"Not really," I admit.

"You told me to tell all those fuckfaces to fuck right off if they couldn't see the talent and brilliance that you see in me," she says with a laugh.

I let go of her hands and scratch the back of my neck.

"Fuckfaces, huh? Real smooth of me."

"It helped. I was so distraught, and it brought a sense of ease."

"I suppose that's good, at least."

I lean back into the corner of the sofa. Cara tucks her legs under her as she leans one arm on the back of it and rests her head on her hand.

"You also told me how great I was in the field. Grant, you have no idea how much you inspired me."

"I thought I was just a thorn in your side," I tease.

"Well, you were certainly that too."

"It was fun tormenting you."

"Oh, believe me, I know you were having a good time when you would get somewhere first or catch the culprit before I arrived."

"Don't act like you didn't find the same sense of victory when it was you."

Cara laughs freely.

"It was nice when it was me one-upping you."

"It was good for me, too, seeing you winning."

"Always on my side."

"What's that?"

Cara sits up straight.

"I never saw it. But you really were always on my side. The whole time."

"I always wanted what was best for you. I saw what you had. I simply played a small part in helping you grow."

Cara leans forward and kisses me softly. As she pulls back, she wraps her arms around my neck as she stays kneeling on the couch.

"You've been here the whole time, and I'm just seeing you now."

I rub her back gently.

"What's important is we both got here."

She kisses me once more before getting back to her original position across from me.

"Can I ask you something else?" she asks.

"You don't have to preface it like that."

"The other night, Noelle told me about something I'd like to talk to you about, but if it's too much, then I understand."

"What is it?"

"She told me about you and Brad and the fire."

I sigh as I scrub my hand down my face.

"She did?"

"Kind of. She didn't go into details. I was hoping you could tell me."

"I'm not trying to hide this from you, but it's a rather simple story."

"I'm listening."

"Brad and I were out one night. I saved his life from a burning building."

Cara gasps, and her eyes widen.

"I know it sounds over-the-top, but Brad really felt like a friend. I probably had gotten too close to him in such a short amount of time, but that's what he was."

"I understand how that could happen."

"I saw the building on fire and knew Brad was in there. I didn't think—I just reacted. Ever since that night, Brad has had a soft spot for our friendship."

"That really..."

"What?"

"Well, that really explains a lot, actually."

"I never meant to hide it from you. It's just complicated. Brad and I both know we shouldn't be friends in any capacity for a multitude of reasons."

"Yet you are."

"Yeah, my love. We are. I can't help it."

Cara smiles at the idea of me having a friendship with Brad. It really was out of place, but it just happened. I wouldn't call it a friendship but a mutual respect, maybe. Either way, I won't dissect it much further. It serves its purpose for both of us in different ways.

"We have to talk about tonight," she says with a sigh.

"The only problem I see in front of us is the code needed right before Taby's quarters."

"You wrote down what you think it is, right?"

"I did. Her assistant did it so quickly though—I don't think we should rely on it."

"I'm good with security systems."

"Believe me, I'm glad you're on my team for this one."

"Me too."

I glance at my watch, and it's a little past three in the afternoon.

"Taby won't be there tonight," Cara says.

"How do you know that?" I ask as I look back up at her.

"I found her schedule in the office. She'll be at a meeting uptown all night. No details on it, but at least we'll be in the clear."

"Outside of her security and guards still there."

"Easy for us."

I chuckle.

"I certainly hope so."

"I think the best time to get there is midnight. Let the place be packed so we can go unnoticed by the guards."

"We'll have to stop the cameras."

"Which means limited time to get through the halls and into her quarters."

"Right."

"Don't worry; that's simple. They'll think it's a glitch if we're less than a minute."

I consider what she's saying. If we're quick, then we could easily get down the halls and into her quarters in that time. The only issue is the code.

"We've got this. You trust me, right?" she asks.

"Implicitly."

SIXTEEN

Cara

I CAN TELL Grant is nervous about tonight. It's not in our skills and abilities, but I think it's because of our relationship status. We're no longer just partners in the field. He looks at me now as if I'm his entire world.

I love it when he does, but it makes me hesitant about his behavior when we're working. The first time I saw the shift in his eyes, my heart melted. I felt like I was in a puddle of happiness after finally finding the one who makes my heart soar.

Grant revs the engine of the car as he switches lanes.

We're both dressed for the mission. He is wearing an all-black suit, and I'm in a matching black suit too. Enough to blend in but also practical for what's to come.

We're silent as he continues to head to the casino.

I've never been a talker in these scenarios, but I usually work alone. I don't know if I should try to be reassuring to Grant or just let him work it out in his head.

"Grant," I say.

"I'm fine."

I laugh.

"Fine? Don't get me started on that obscene excuse for a word again."

Grant smirks and glances over at me before focusing back on the road.

"I love you. That's all. I've never had someone I love be in danger before. It's something I have to work through, but I know it's a *me* issue."

"We've got this. We'll both be fine. This is a simple recon mission to find out what we need to know. Time is passing by, and we don't have a clue who the Marlin is."

"I know."

"Something has to be in Taby's quarters."

"I agree. It's too personal for there not to be."

"Good."

Grant pulls into a spot by the side of the casino near a back door. It's still around other cars but will be near the closest exit we can take to leave quickly.

We both hop out of the car and silently walk into the casino. Spotting the private room, we give our names to the guard, who sees we are permanent guests on the list to get in.

Simple already. We won't be tracked necessarily, and if anything, our being here should look good if Cordelia or Taby were to find out. We're coming back to the business and showing our support without work being involved.

It's going to plan, and that's all that matters. Simple and easy. Grant has nothing to be worried about.

We saunter past the gamblers and revelers as we make our way to one of the bars. We'll stake out here for a bit before making our move.

"What can I get for you?" the bartender asks.

"Tonic with lime, please."

"Make that two."

"Two tonics with limes coming right up," he answers.

Leaning with my back to the bar, I look around the casino to make sure there's no one here who would immediately recognize us. Grant does the same, facing the bar area.

"I think we're good," I tell Grant.

"No one on the opposite side either."

"Perfect."

"Here you go," the bartender says as he slides the drinks over.

Grant pays in cash and turns to hand me mine.

"Thank you."

"Cheers."

We clink glasses and keep observing the room.

"There are four cameras on the door that will be an issue."

"Then I clocked six cameras in the route there."

"That's not bad," I say.

"Not at all."

Grant and I both hold onto our drinks to blend in with the crowd.

"Ready?" he asks.

"Let's go. We'll set these down over there," I answer while pointing to a table of discarded drinks.

We meander over in that direction, trying to act as naturally as possible. Almost simultaneously, we set the full glasses down on the table.

I pull out a device and start tapping away.

"That's how the cameras will be cut?"

"Yes."

A few more taps and bingo.

"Ready, in three, two, one. Cut."

I press the button that shuts down all the cameras in the casino. Grant and I close the distance to the door and type in the code quickly. The commotion of the cameras being off allows us to slip in undetected.

Guards around the room are being notified in their earpieces that something is up. As the door closes behind us, the adrenaline kicks in.

We run down the hallways as fast as we can and finally reach the destination. Dozens of red lasers cross every which way to the door.

"Try the code," I say.

Grant enters it, and nothing happens.

"Try something else."

Grant types in another code, but nothing happens again.

"What's the plan?" he asks.

"I've got this," I say.

I pull out another device and hook it up to the control panel.

"Time is almost up," Grant says.

I push a few buttons, and it starts to run numbers on it.

"It's almost been a minute," Grant says.

Four. Seven. Two. Six.

And they're off.

"Run," I shout.

We both sprint down the hall to the door. I use a hairpin to unlock the door, and we slam it shut behind us.

"Fuck," I whisper, out of breath.

"We did it. Fifty-six seconds."

"Good. That's good. Now we only have a few minutes

until guards come searching in here to make sure there are no intruders. Where do you think she keeps her documents?"

Grant scans the room and settles on a door near the bar area.

"In there. Cordelia was in that room while I was here. It has to be important."

We dart across the room and into a hidden oasis. A stream flows through it, and there is greenery everywhere.

"Wasn't expecting this," he murmurs.

"I'll say."

"Over there." He points across the room.

I spot the same discreet-looking decorative cabinet. It looks out of place in this room.

Grant opens it up, and there's a large safe sitting in it. I hook up the same device to try and crack the code.

"What is this thing?" Grant asks.

"Our ticket to information."

"Fair enough."

The numbers run again, and it gives me the code.

"Does this work for everything?"

I laugh.

"Yes."

"Can I get one?" he teases.

"Later, Sinclair."

"I like it when you boss me around."

I roll my eyes as I punch in the code.

"Alright. Here we go!" he says.

Opening it up, we find a thick file.

A search through the documents reveals numerous players in the operation. Grant holds the files out as I snap a picture of each one. As he flips through them, I realize that this really is it.

"Wait," I whisper.

He pauses mid-flip.

"This is... this is it."

Grant holds the paper in front of him and scans it.

"You're right."

"Quick, let me take a photo."

He puts it back in front of me, and I snap a photo of the page and the remaining few after that too.

"Let's get out of here," I say.

Grant nods, puts the file back, and shuts everything closed once again the way it was.

"How are we leaving the room?" he asks.

"Shutting it all down again."

Grant cocks an eyebrow.

"Well, it works," I answer.

"I'll follow your lead."

I pull out the same device as we head out.

"Three, two, one."

I cut the cameras and then enter the code to turn off the lasers from the opposite direction.

We dart down the hallways quickly and finally arrive back at the main entrance to the offices and private quarters. Grant peeks out the door and gives me a signal that it's all clear again.

Walking as fast as we can, we leave the casino without anyone knowing what we just did.

"I can't believe that worked."

"I can. You're brilliant," he counters.

We both slide into the car, and Grant starts the engine immediately.

"Let's get home, Sinclair."

BACK AT THE HOUSE, I print all the photos right away. Grant has coffees prepared in the dining room and a pinboard out for us to start reviewing our findings.

"Okay, here we go," I say, coming into the room and holding out a stack of photographs.

"Let's sort them by the players, the plan, and..." Grant trails off.

"What's wrong?"

"It's nothing."

"Grant, now's not the time to be hiding anything."

He studies me as I set down the photos on the table.

"The price. With all the names we scanned, don't you think that this is bigger than what we imagined?"

"Yes, it's possible. Of course it is."

"All of this for diamonds? I don't believe it for a second."

"You're underestimating one major factor in all of this."

"What's that?"

"Greed. I know to you and me, it seems questionable why diamonds, or even drugs and other illegal trading, would be worth it, but it all adds up. It is worth it to people like Taby and Cordelia, who want more and are never satisfied. It'll be worth it to the Marlin too."

"You're right. They are the company she keeps."

"Exactly."

"I think it's time we call Dodger for another check-in. He's going to want to know about all of this."

"It's a lot."

"Which is good for us."

"Hopefully, he agrees."

Grant takes out his cell phone and dials the agency. An assistant transfers Grant to Dodger's office.

"I'm on hold," he whispers to me.

I give him a small nod as I start to organize the photographs into their respective categories.

Studying all the people who are part of this is everything we needed to confirm our original intel. People from all over the country funneling money, drugs, diamonds, and more into the Carolinas mafia operation.

All because of the Marlin.

"This is Sinclair and Collins here," Grant says as he puts the phone on the table.

"It's on speaker," he mouths to me.

"Great. What do you have for me?" Dodger asks.

"We have confirmed intel about all the key players in the Carolinas mafia operation. We're sorting through the documents with full details now. Tomorrow night, Sinclair is participating in an undercover operation that we think is connected to what we have here."

"Good. When you have more, let me know."

"Will do, sir," I answer.

"We'll want to move in immediately as the Marlin is confirmed."

"Understood."

The phone call ends without another word. Grant pockets his cell phone.

"It's going to be a long night." I sigh.

"Let's keep at it."

Grant starts pinning the sorted photographs to the pinboard as I separate them into categories.

"Hey, Sinclair?"

"Yeah, Collins?"

"I'm glad I'm with you during these long nights."

He gives me one of his breathtaking smiles.

"Me too."

We get to work, going back and forth with theories and dissecting all the details we've found.

What we know is that sometime in the next week, there's going to be a major meetup at a warehouse in Charlotte.

"Brad has to know."

"Will he tell you?"

Grant runs a hand through his hair as he paces in front of the board. I stretch in my seat with my arms over my head.

"No. Brad may have warned me about all of this in a way, but he won't tell me anything about this meetup."

"What about Fred?"

"Fred?" he asks, confused.

"Yes, the guy from the barbecue."

"Oh right, how could I forget."

"What do you mean?"

"He tried to provoke me that day."

"How so?"

Grant chuckles in disbelief.

"He said he wanted to taste your pie."

"That's so cheesy and odd to say."

"Yeah. I wasn't exactly pleased about it."

As I settle back into my seat, realization dawns on me.

"Okay, that aside, he doesn't seem very..."

I pause, debating how to word this.

"But he's... How do I say this?"

Grant crosses his arms over his chest and leans against a nearby wall. The exhaustion is apparent.

"Don't go getting polite on me now about this."

"Very funny."

I stand to stretch my legs and pace in front of him now.

"He's not very smart. Like really, you know?"

"I would have to agree with that."

"So wouldn't someone like that write down where the meeting is taking place so they wouldn't forget? I mean, he probably doesn't think anyone would break into his house to get this kind of intel."

Grant uncrosses his arms and studies me.

"You're right."

"So maybe we need to do a little break-in? Find out if he has written down the date, time, and location."

"It's too much," Grant counters.

"It's not. We need these details."

"I might get them from Taby after I win tomorrow night."

"You won't."

"Why do you say that?"

"It's too soon to bring you in like this. Isn't it?"

Grant turns away, putting his back to me as he examines the board.

"You know I'm right."

"Saturday. I'll ask Brad and Fred to come over for drinks, and you can go in there. At least that way, we know he's definitely not home."

I wrap my arms around Grant's waist from behind and rest my head on his back.

"It'll work."

"I know you're right. Doesn't mean I have to like it."

I take a deep breath and rest my eyes.

"I have to win tomorrow night."

"You do."

"Taby or her goons might kill me if I don't."

"But you will."

"Taby needs those diamonds, and I'm going to make it

happen. When I hand them over, she'll have to tell me why. I'll make her."

I chuckle.

"You are mister charming."

"As long as you're my lucky charm, I have no worries about that."

SEVENTEEN

Grant

"THIS IS GRANT," I say, answering my cell phone.

"Look what that cat dragged in."

I chuckle as I finish putting on my tuxedo for tonight.

"How are you doing, old man?"

"Better now that I finally hear back from you," Luke says.

"It's been a while."

"Ages. When are you coming back to California?"

"Soon. A few weeks at most."

"Cara told me something similar."

I can sense the hesitation in my friend's voice. There's no way he thinks we're connected, yet both of us being absent during the same time frame is rather suspicious.

"I'm sure she'll be back before me. How's she doing?"

Luke sighs.

"Good. Fine. I don't get much out of her when she's working."

"I'm sure she would tell you if you needed to worry."

"Maybe..." He trails off.

"Well, tell me when you're back in town. We'll have to have you over for dinner or go golfing. Hell, both," he says with a chuckle.

"Will do. Take care of yourself."

"You too."

I end the call and put the phone in my inner jacket pocket.

"Everything okay?" Cara's sweet voice asks from behind.

She takes my breath away, standing in my doorway. We've been sleeping together in her original bedroom, but I've still kept my clothes in a separate room.

"Good. Just talked to your dad, actually."

Cara gives me a surprised look.

"We'll have to figure that out eventually. Not now."

"No, definitely not now," she muses.

"He said you haven't shared much with him."

"Don't do this, Grant." She sighs.

"Your dad just wants to make sure you're okay. When did you talk to him?"

"Maybe an hour ago. He called as I was getting ready. I hadn't answered him the past few times."

"I won't pry. He just loves you."

"I know. I'll do better. Sounds like you should too."

"You're right."

"I usually am," she says with a waggle of her eyebrows. I chuckle as I search for my watch.

"I'll meet you downstairs," I say.

"Okay, I love you."

"And I love you."

I walk over to her with my watch in hand and place a kiss on the top of her head.

"Are you sure you're okay?" she asks.

"I promise."

She hesitantly leaves the room.

I am fine. I wouldn't lie to Cara, but talking to Luke, albeit briefly, was strange given how much has changed for Cara and me.

It's time to focus on the game ahead of us. Tonight is one of the last steps we'll have to take to finally get the Marlin.

I finish putting on my watch and take a last look in the mirror.

"Ready or not."

THE TOURNAMENT ISN'T EXACTLY as I pictured it would be. It's nothing like the one that Taby had hosted. As I stand in front of this dingy building, I debate taking off parts of my tuxedo.

It's by the coast, so I can hear the faint sound of the waves crashing in the distance. The smell of the sea is prevalent, and I try to place where the beach is from here. It's late, making it too dark to really be able to see my surroundings well.

"Everything okay?" Cara's sweet voice sounds in my earpiece.

"Good. Just taking it all in."

"It's different than what I imagined."

"Me too."

I pause as I see someone dressed down going through the entrance of the building.

"I need to rethink this tuxedo."

"Maybe just put your bow tie in your pocket," she suggests.

"Good thinking."

I quickly undo my bow tie and put it in my jacket pocket. I'm still in a nice-looking suit, but hopefully, it'll come across as less over-the-top than with it.

"I'm going in. Taking this out for the time being."

"I don't think you should do that."

"I'm probably going to be swept or, at the very least, checked going in here. This doesn't seem like the most trusting of venues."

"Okay. I'll be out here in the car waiting. Please keep me posted as you can."

"Will do, love."

Taking out my earpiece, I try to hide it on the back of my cell phone. It won't be suspicious if that goes off. Technology glitch or something of the sort.

As I walk up the set of dirty steps, I bang on the broken steel door. Someone looks through a glass opening right away and gives me a once-over.

The person backs away, and only moments later, the door is being cracked open. I step inside the dark room as the person shuts it behind me. It rings through the room as the door struggles to shut.

"Ace Weston. Here to play in the poker tournament."

The man looks at me with a blank expression. I keep eye contact as I wait for any signal of what's to come.

"Through the hall, door is straight ahead," the bouncer says.

"Thanks."

I give him a tilt of my head as I start to head toward the

tournament. Suddenly, the door opens, and I turn back around to see who it is. Someone I don't recognize, who looks worse for wear. He's sporting an all-black outfit but looks weathered and exhausted.

Time to focus on what's ahead.

As I go through the doors, I walk into a room full of chatter coming from every inch of the place. There are people seated in rows around the poker table smack dab in the center of it all.

The adrenaline rush that I feel when on a mission comes flooding through my nervous system.

I spot other players gathered near the poker table, so I head toward them.

"Ace Weston?" someone asks as I approach.

"That's me."

"Bucky. This here is my tournament. Cordelia or Taby tell you the rules of my game?"

"Afraid not."

His gut spills over the top of his pants, which he starts to pull up. Bucky. He's sweating profusely as he signals for all the other players to gather round.

The man who came in behind me steps next to where I wait.

"Roberts?"

"Joe Roberts."

"Good. Just in time; otherwise, you would have been eliminated," Bucky says.

"Here are the rules of my game. No buy-ins once you're out. If you're caught counting or cheating in any way, you're out and forfeit your spot. That goes for tonight and the next year. Hell, for fuckin' ever. Got it?" Bucky asks.

Everyone agrees to the terms.

"One winner. Tonight, you'll be paid in diamonds that you can turn into cash. I don't fuckin' care what you do with them."

The group of players nods in agreement.

"Good. Drinks are on the house after this. Let the game begin," he finishes and signals for the dealer to approach the table.

We all take our seats, and as soon as I sit, I notice someone I've seen before since being in North Carolina. Maybe from a barbecue or the casino, but one of these players is connected to Taby's organization. I feel it in my gut.

All these people around me must be part of some kind of criminal organization. This isn't exactly the most welcoming crowd to step into.

I'm nervous that Cara is outside waiting. Once again, I have to remind myself that she's used to being in these situations. Just because I want to protect her doesn't mean I can stifle who she is.

One by one, the dealer starts to deal the poker cards, and the first game is underway minutes later.

With the tournament stretching on, I use all my skills to stay in it. Player after player is being taken out, and I can't get overly confident with what's happening. All it takes is one slip, and I'll lose.

"Roberts. Weston. Final round."

Roberts looks up at me, but I can't make out his expression as he keeps a stoic look plastered on and wears his cap and matching glasses.

The dealer deals out the cards, and I keep my sunglasses on to hide any sign of concern from my eyes.

Roberts raises the bet. I follow next, back and forth, until it's up to him to go once again.

His head tilts up for the first time since the start of this round. I still can't make out his expression. Does he have a winning hand? I'm really not sure what to make of this. Roberts is a professional, that much is clear, and I'm not just talking about cards. There's more to his story than he's letting on.

A small tap on the cards tells me he's made his decision. He displays his cards, and as I do the same, the results are right there—I've won.

Roberts stands and comes around to my side of the table. I get up to shake his hand. Around us, the crowd is loud, and it's hard to hear what Roberts said or what the dealer announced.

Suddenly, Bucky is right by my side, pulling me as he shouts to the crowd that I won his tournament and the ultimate prize.

"Come with me," he murmurs as he guides me into a back set of offices.

He stomps on, huffing, and I focus on getting the diamonds so that I can get them to Taby. That's the goal. Show her I can win and hopefully find out more.

Bucky busts through a dirty door with broken blinds, and I freeze in the doorway. A woman with bright-red lips and a fake tan is giving me a smug look with a box in front of her on the desk.

"Well done, Ace."

I stand there in shock.

"Don't look so surprised."

I take a step back.

"Aria."

"In the flesh. Looks like you won my tournament."

She leans back in her chair with her legs kicked out in front of her.

"Your tournament?"

"Why? Is it so odd that a woman can be in charge?"

"It's not," I interject.

"Good. That would be bad for me to report to Taby."

"Why did Bucky claim this was his tournament?"

"He's just my manager. Handles the day-to-day while I'm off playing with everyone else."

"Fair enough."

"Are you to be trusted?" she asks with a cock of her head.

"I hope so."

"Don't we all."

"What do you mean by that?"

"So many questions for someone so new."

I don't answer.

"New people are dangerous in the games we play. I'm surprised, that's all."

"Well, I hope you can trust me."

"Don't worry about me," she answers.

I give her a nod as I stand tall with my hands behind my back and feet spread apart.

"Here you go. All the diamonds that Taby is expecting as part of the transaction."

"As part of my winnings."

"Precisely. All clean. Now it's in your hands if there are issues as to where the diamonds came from, not Taby's."

"Or yours."

Aria laughs darkly as she stands and walks toward me.

"You're such a good boy. Very clever. Taby couldn't risk losing me or having my hands dirty."

She pauses and then opens the door wider.

"Well, not with this, at least."

Aria stands next to the fully open door and raises her eyebrows.

"Better get those to Taby. She doesn't like to wait."

"I was planning on going tomorrow."

Aria laughs again.

"I'd get them to her tonight. But what do I know? I've just lived to tell the tale for years."

I take the box and head out through the door. As I go toward the main poker space, Roberts comes out from a different door and grins.

He works for Aria. He was a plant to try and make me lose. I don't fully understand what's at play here, but one thing is for sure—we're in deep.

BACK IN THE CAR, Cara screeches out of the parking lot as soon as I hop in. As she takes a corner, she looks down to see the box I'm holding.

"You won." She beams.

"I did. Barely."

"Barely?"

She shifts gears and zooms past a set of cars.

"The owner is Aria."

"What?" she asks, shocked.

"And Aria planted someone there. Someone good. To beat me."

"Wow," she answers in disbelief.

"Tell me about it. He was a professional. Now I know at least that I've seen him before."

"You recognized him?"

"I did. I couldn't place it, and frankly, I still can't, but he had to have been at the casino the other night."

"It's amazing how intricate all of this is. What a web they've woven."

I sigh and shut my eyes in the passenger seat.

"Hopefully, this pleases Taby."

"It will. I'm sure of it."

Cara hops onto the highway and heads back to Charlotte.

"Where to?" she asks.

"Taby's casino. Aria recommended I get this to her immediately."

"And we trust Aria's opinion?"

"If I were a betting man, I would say not, but I'd rather attempt it tonight."

"Okay. You're the lead with this," she says.

Opening my eyes, I look over to see a fierce and determined Cara driving as fast as she can to get us home.

The way her hair flows through the air makes me want to just watch her the whole ride home. If only I didn't need some rest ahead of the meeting with Taby.

I reach over and take one of her hands off the steering wheel and intertwine it with mine.

"Better?" she asks with a wide smile.

"Much."

"Get some rest, Grant. You'll need it."

"I will. It's just hard to not be so distracted by your beauty."

Cara shakes her head, but that smile stays firmly in place.

"Get some sleep. We'll be there in less than an hour."

"My lucky charm."

"YOU DID WELL, ACE," Taby says in a pleased tone.

"Happy to be of assistance."

Taby is sitting in her primary office tonight. I keep standing near the doorway, next to a guard who came in with me. The casino is lively, with an up-and-coming pop star, Luna Stone, performing.

For a mafia operation, the front is the best one I've ever seen. Taby's casino is the place in Charlotte to be seen.

Taby tents her fingers over her mouth and stares while I try to stay as calm and collected as I can. She is debating bringing me into the fold after I was able to successfully bring the diamonds back.

She leans back in her chair while keeping her eyes firmly on me.

"Did Aria try to prevent you from winning?"

"I didn't see Aria until I won."

Taby laughs darkly.

"That's not what I asked."

Moment of truth.

"Yes. I believe so."

"And what did she do exactly?"

"There was another player there who I believe was a plant. He was good. Clearly a professional poker player. He came in second place."

'What was this man's name?"

"Joe. Joe Roberts."

Taby gestures for the guard next to me to come over to her. She whispers something in his ear, and he leaves the office immediately. She brings her attention back to me.

"Aria is a complication that will be dealt with."

I swallow thickly. I need Taby's trust, but it's against my better judgment to want someone to die in this situation.

"I thought it was a test. From you."

"Possibly."

She's not going to tell me what's happening. Taby opens a drawer and pulls out a stack of money.

"Here's your cut for tonight," she says as she slides it over.

I take it off her desk and pocket it.

"Thank you."

"I have another proposition for you."

This is it.

"Cordelia, well, she's cautious about you and your wife. Should she be?"

"No."

"Good. If there's a problem, you know what will happen to you?"

Death.

"Yes."

"Good."

Taby shuffles through the same drawer and pulls out an envelope.

"Next week, we have a meeting. I'll need someone to distribute some goods quickly. Can you do that?"

"Yes."

"This is yours for now. Once you complete it, you'll get the rest."

I take the envelope and see it's packed with hundred-dollar bills.

"If it's this important, should I go to the meeting?"

Taby's eyes narrow.

"I don't think that's necessary."

"Whatever you say, boss."

"Someone will be in touch."

I take that as my cue to leave.

As I head back to a waiting Cara in the car, I realize that

Taby let a truth slip in there. Cordelia doesn't trust us for some reason. If Cordelia is Taby's right-hand woman, then I need her to trust us.

There has to be something we can do if it becomes necessary. At least until then, Cara and I need to try and fly under the radar unless Fred's house comes up as a dead end.

Tomorrow, we'll know what our game plan has to be.

EIGHTEEN

Cara

WITH THE RECENT events that have transpired, we're putting it all on the line, assuming Fred has been careless. That he is as foolish as we think he is and will have the information somewhere in his home.

I know in my gut that I'm right about this. I have to be.

Staring out the front window, I wait for Fred and Brad to come over. I cross my arms and pace in front of it in hopes that one of them will arrive soon.

I've set up a whole spread of dishes for them to eat, arranged different types of beers, and we even subscribed to a new channel to get the game. We know that, locally, everyone roots for the Stingrays, a Charleston-based team.

"You don't have to do this," Grant says.

My head snaps over to where he waits against the bottom of the staircase. He's dressed casually in a green, long-sleeved Henley and a pair of dark jeans.

"And you look delicious," I say.

He smiles briefly, but it doesn't reach his eyes.

"I'm serious, Cara. Let me figure out a different way to break into Fred's. I'm sure I could even convince him to just invite me over."

I let out a long sigh and stop pacing altogether.

"We're out of time, Grant. You know this."

"We can figure it out. I don't feel right about you going over there. Not with the way Fred's looked at you and that pie comment."

"He's harmless," I counter.

"But we don't actually know that. Nothing is what we assumed it would be when we first got here. Look at Aria. Did you see that coming?"

Okay, well, he has a good point there. I didn't see that one coming.

"Exactly," he finishes.

"I'll be gone for only a few minutes. In and out. I won't search his whole house. I won't have to. Don't you see? It'll be easy."

"Easy," he says, drawing it out.

"Yes."

"I won't stop you, but I don't have to like it."

"We're so close. As soon as we get the meetup information, this will all be over. The Marlin will be there, and we'll finally catch whoever it is."

"At this rate, the Marlin is probably a woman."

"I don't even pretend to know who it could be. Like you said, nothing is what it seems here."

"Okay. I'll trust you. Please just be careful."

"I will be. I'm good at my job."

"I never said you weren't. I'm allowed to be worried about you."

"I love you."

"I love you." He sighs and then gets a startled look, peering around me through the open window.

"THEY'RE HERE. You better go out the back."

I turn around and see Brad and Fred walking up our driveway together. They look like they're having an intense conversation that no doubt has something to do with next week.

"I'll be back before you know it, and I'll keep an eye out for Fred."

Grant sighs as he walks toward the front door, then pauses next to me.

"Go."

"I love you," I repeat.

"And I love you."

I take off in a sprint through the living room and kitchen to the back patio door. We have a walkway around the side of the house that will lead me in the right direction to Fred's house.

I pass through a set of tall hedges and pause next to the front porch. I hear Grant welcoming them into the home. Moments go by, and the door is shut.

Looking around the neighborhood, I try to quickly dart across the way to Fred's. There's no one out walking right now, which is strange but lucky.

Maybe I am a lucky charm for myself too.

I get to the back of Fred's house and pull out my lock-pick in case I need it. Testing a door handle, I wiggle it, and the door opens. It's unlocked.

I scan my surroundings and slip inside, shutting the door quietly behind me.

This house has a similar layout to ours, so I know right away which direction I want to go.

The office is on the first floor, off the living room. It's almost an open concept with large glass doors. Spotting it, I feel a sense of victory that I was right.

In Fred's office, there's a huge stack of papers strewn across his desk. Who even prints this much these days?

I get settled in his seat and start going through the documents.

Nothing related to the meetup at the warehouse.

I chew the inside of my mouth as I debate where to go next.

His bedroom or a guest bedroom, perhaps. This house is far too big for a single man to live in. I'm surprised that he hasn't moved a girlfriend in just to not feel so lonely.

I take the stairs as fast as I can, running on the adrenaline that's coursing through every inch of me.

I decide to head into one of the spare rooms first.

As I open the door, I'm hit with an overwhelming sense of dread. Inside this room are dozens of computers and various security measures, from the looks of it.

"Fuck," I mutter.

Scanning the screens on one of the walls, I recognize the inside of this house mainly, but then I spot something that stops me in my tracks. There is live security camera footage from inside the casino.

I'm in shock as I watch these feeds. Only I don't think Fred has Taby's permission to do this. This must be why Fred moved to the neighborhood. He's not in on it all like I thought he might be.

He arrived only months before we did, but the way Brad talked to him made me feel like he was a bigger player in the operation. Now I'm not so sure.

Why would he be doing this unless he had an ulterior motive of some kind? I won't even pretend to know what that could be.

Stepping forward to one particular screen, I see Taby and Cordelia lounging at a table inside Taby's private quarters.

Taby definitely doesn't know that Fred has this on her. There's no way she would allow this with all the security measures she has in place at the casino. Fred might be part of her organization, but there's no way that he's this involved to have access to her this way.

Reaching for my cell phone, I take photos of the monitors first and then the computers. There's data on them that must be important to Taby.

There's a tablet on the table that has a passcode on it. I try a few typical codes but don't get in.

"There has to be something here," I say to myself.

While looking for any sign of a password, my eyes land on a picture of Fred from high school or college. He and his three friends are all holding up a sign for something. A fraternity, perhaps.

2006.

The year he graduated college.

I enter it into his tablet, and it opens up. Scrolling through it, I find a note icon and click it. I scan through the notes and see they're labeled by dates. I open each one for next week to try and find the answers we're looking for.

One last one to try, I open the note.

Milton Warehouse District.

Fourth and Third.

8 p.m.

The note date is only a couple of days away.

I'm filled with relief for successfully finding the information we need.

Putting the tablet back in its place, I take a photo of the note before turning it off completely.

I quietly walk past the computer monitors and open up one of the laptops. I need to find a way to shut off and erase any record that I've been here.

Thankfully, I find access immediately and erase everything from the past fifteen minutes. Then I take a deep breath and shut off the cameras.

I have no time at all to get out of here. Hopefully, Fred won't notice since he's watching the game at my house.

I slip out of the office and slowly shut the door behind me so there's no proof I was there. Feeling accomplished, I smile at all my findings.

Suddenly, a rough hand is at my throat, and I'm dying to find air. I struggle against the person's hold as my eyes sting with water from the way he's holding onto my neck.

"Well, well, well, look at what we have here," the man says.

His tone is laced with menace and desire as he continues to hold me tight.

"What are you doing in my house, baby?"

My eyes clear, and I realize it's Fred. He must have left my house. Only there's no way Grant knows because he would have come with him to warn me.

Fred releases his hand from around my neck, and I gasp for air.

"I asked you a question."

I grip my neck as I try to inhale as much air as I can. Fred is strong, much stronger than I assumed he would be. I'm beginning to realize there's a lot I don't know about Fred Jones.

"I-I..." I stutter.

I didn't anticipate being caught in the act by him. I've rarely been in this situation with some of the worst criminals in the world.

"Oh, baby, looks like you found out my secret," he says.

The camera room.

"What am I going to do with you now?"

"I swear, I wasn't in there. I came over to find out a few things that you like for Grant. He wanted to surprise you since your birthday is coming up. Have a party with friends," I lie.

Fred takes a step back and examines me. The way his deep-blue eyes try to peer into mine is alarming. I've never taken a good look at Fred before, but his tall, broad frame is powerful next to mine. The way his tattoos travel up the length of his arms tells a story I don't think I want to know.

"What did you see? Don't lie to me," he says. It comes out harshly, as though he's worried about whether to believe me or not.

"Nothing. Just technology. But I mean, everyone has computers?"

Fred crosses his arms and leans against his staircase railing.

"You've come snooping in another man's home looking like you wanted to be caught."

I look down at my attire, and confusion fills me. I'm not in anything sexy, not that it would be my fault if I did choose to dress that way. He needs to be able to keep it in his pants, even if I were wearing underwear over here.

"I'm wearing leather pants and a shirt?"

"Your tits are basically popping out of your shirt, baby. You come here dressed like that, looking around my bedrooms. Makes me feel like you want something you aren't getting at home."

I stand tall yet pretend to be bashful as he tries to come onto me. A meek little housewife who needs attention from her neighbor.

Fred uncrosses his arms and stalks forward. He reaches for me and gently starts caressing my neck with his fingers. It's no where near the roughness as before.

"What are you doing?" I whisper.

"Can you keep a secret?" he huskily asks.

Fuck. I cannot sleep with Fred. I need to attack him and leave, then tell Grant, and we can clean up the mess together.

Being in a relationship changes everything. Ordinarily, I would have probably given in a little, just enough to tempt him into letting me leave. I can't put Grant's and my relationship at risk.

"Of course," I say with an innocent smile in place.

Maybe if I hit him right on the nose and kick him in the groin, it will take him down.

"I won't tell anyone that you were getting up to no good in another man's house if we can keep a secret."

"From Ace?"

"From everyone, baby. I can fuck you so good that you'll want to come over here day and night to get some from your neighbor Fred."

My breath hitches as he steps almost flush to my body. It's now or never. I have to get out of here before this happens.

Out of the corner of my eye, I see a figure slowly coming up the stairs.

Grant.

He climbs each step as Fred focuses on me.

"Come on, baby, what do you say? Let me fuck you right now. I promise it'll be better than what he gives you," Fred continues.

"Is that so?" Grant says.

Fred takes a surprised step back and staggers in the opposite direction from where Grant approaches.

I let out a relieved breath of air and feel my heart beating wildly in my chest. Grant looks over at me as he passes.

"Did he touch you?" he asks.

"Just my neck."

A tick appears in his jaw as his eyes darken and set course for Fred once again.

"What were you saying to my wife?"

"Nothing. It was nothing. Just messing with her." Fred stumbles over his words.

Grant hums thoughtfully.

"Messing with her."

"Yeah, that's all. She was snooping in my house, and I know it's not for some fucking birthday party."

"It was."

Grant towers over Fred. All the blood drains from Fred's face as he waits for Grant's next move.

"You're so interested in my wife," Grant says.

"I'm not."

Grant cocks an eyebrow and looks back at me. A devilish smile takes over.

"You're not? I recall you saying you wanted a piece of her pie."

Oh no. Grant might actually kill him.

Grant picks Fred up by his shoulders and slams him against the hallway wall.

"I don't want anything from her," Fred cries out.

"Now who's lying?" Grant chuckles.

I wrap my arms around Grant's waist as he holds onto Fred.

"Ace, don't do this."

Grant looks over his shoulder at me.

"All I see is his blood spilling everywhere. He touched you."

Grant looks back at Fred.

"And she's not yours to fucking touch."

Tension is rolling off Grant in waves as he debates killing Fred, and I realize I need to intervene. I don't know what comes over me, but as wetness starts to pool in my panties from watching Grant claim me as his, only one idea comes to mind.

"Ace, sweetie. Why don't you show him that I'm yours?" I offer.

The words slip out of my mouth without a second thought. I'm getting damper by the second since saying it, and I realize that I want nothing more than for Grant to show his possessive side and fuck me in front of Fred.

Grant slowly turns his head back to me.

"What are you saying?"

"I'm saying, why don't you tie our friend Fred up and fuck me like you own me."

Grant's eyes slowly change from a look of murder to lust.

"I do own you."

"Then prove it."

Grant's jaw tightens as his cock hardens in his pants.

"I don't want him to see you naked."

"He'll be dead by tomorrow with what I found," I whisper.

Grant brings Fred down to the ground and loosens his

grip around his neck. Fred tries to struggle free of his hold. In an instant, Grant takes Fred's head in his hand and slams it back into the wall, leaving a giant hole in its wake.

With his grip still on his head and Fred's blood dripping everywhere, Grant pushes him through the open bedroom door, then shoves him onto the bed face-first.

"Get me ties."

I shuffle through Fred's closet and find a set of ties that should do the job. Scurrying out of the closet, I hand one of them over to Grant, who uses it to tie Fred's hands together behind his back. He takes another one and wraps it around Fred's mouth to prevent him from talking.

"One more, my love," Grant says to me.

I hand him one more and toss the others to the ground. Grant uses it to tie Fred's feet to a bedpost.

Fred is frantically trying to get out of the holds.

"Pants down. Ass up," Grant says to me.

My eyes shoot up in surprise. I've never seen this side of Grant, and I like it. This is the badass secret agent whom I had heard so much about.

I pull my pants to my ankles.

"Actually, shirt too."

I didn't want Fred to see me naked, yet right now, all I want is to be fucked by Grant any way he'll have me.

I pull my shirt overhead and set it on the bed. Grant's eyes simmer with desire as he stares at my chest.

His eyes go from me to Fred, and I follow his line of sight. Fred has stopped his struggling and is watching me undress.

"Do you like what you see? Cara's perfect tits ready to be played with."

Instinctually, I reach behind my back and unhook my

bra. I let it fall to the ground, leaving my breasts hanging free.

Fred groans as he stares at them.

Grant looks over at me and grins. It's a different, more sadistic side of the usually pulled-together man I've fallen in love with. I realize now that I love every side of Grant that I get to experience.

I want him to own me in front of Fred.

I've never been shy about my body. It's helped me numerous times out in the field. I'll do whatever Grant says. He would never make me do anything I didn't want. And right now? Right now, I like that I'm watching desire swirl in Fred's eyes.

I like feeling wanted by both of the men in the room.

Grant steps back over to me and bends down to be at eye level with my chest. He squeezes my breasts together and presses his face between them.

He starts lapping them up, and I pull at his hair, enjoying every second of it. My head falls back as I hold onto Grant for dear life while he licks and nips at my nipples.

Grant pulls away, and I instantly feel the loss. He grins and bends down fully, taking my panties with him. They hang at my ankles with my pants.

He pulls them off, and I'm standing naked in front of Grant and Fred.

"Turn around. Hands on the bed. Follow the rules, my pretty wife," Grant says.

I do as he says and place my hands on the bed right next to where Fred's sitting quietly. My breasts hang from this position, and I notice the way Fred is watching them intently.

I jut my ass out, and Grant instantly grazes it with one of his palms.

"My perfect little whore of a wife," Grant murmurs as he continues to tease my ass.

"Yes," I moan.

"Do you want me to fuck you in front of Fred? Should I show him who you belong to, *wife*?"

"Yes," I whimper, needing more.

My pussy is soaked from the teasing that Grant delivers. I hear Grant pull down his pants and a shuffling as they get moved to the side.

Grant grips one of my hips as he uses the other to line up his cock with my entrance. He pushes inside, and I feel the intrusion immediately.

"Oh god, yes," I shout.

Grant begins to thrust rapidly as he holds onto both of my hips and rocks me roughly into the bed. I try to hold onto the blanket for any kind of balance. Fred's blood is mixed into the sheets, and I have no idea if that's where I'm holding.

"Do you wish you were the one fucking her?" Grant asks Fred as he continues thrusting.

Fred stays silent, but I look over to see him painfully hard.

"Ace, baby. Fred's about to come in his pants."

"I don't care. Let him."

"Ace," I repeat.

Grant stills for a moment, understanding. I may be his wife, whom he's crazy about in real life, but in this world, we need to keep Fred alive as part of the bigger picture today. Grant can't kill him, no matter how much he wants to.

In the real world, we are the good guys, and in this

world, we may be bad, but in order to tell Taby what he's done, we have no choice but to turn this situation around.

"Fred. Do you get the picture here?"

Fred nods his head up and down.

"Will you be coming onto my wife again?"

Fred tries to say something as he shakes his head no in return.

Grant reaches forward and grabs my tits in his hands, pulling me more upright than I was. I reach my arms back and try to tangle them into Grant's hair.

"I'm yours," I whisper into his ear.

"You're in control. Not me," he whispers back.

God, I have never felt more desired and heated than I do in this moment.

"Fucking hell," Grant shouts.

He pulls out of me and walks over, hard cock and all, to Fred. He pulls off his binds from his hands first, then his feet from the bedpost. Fred pulls down the binding in his mouth and resumes his seat.

"We're good, right?" Grant grits out.

Fred undoes his pants and pulls out his weeping cock. Grant pushes me against the bed, and I feel like I'm about to come just from this alone.

Grant spreads my legs apart and slams his cock back inside me, pulling my hips to move me forward. My hair is sprawled against the bed as I become a sweaty mess.

My breasts are bouncing freely as Grant continues his familiar rough thrusts.

"Fuck, this is something else," Fred finally says.

His cock is in his hand as he watches Grant fuck me. Seeing him stroke his cock to Grant and me fucking is exhilarating.

Grant begins to palm my clit when he feels me contracting around his cock.

"That's it, my slutty wife. You like watching Fred fucking his palm to you, don't you?"

"Yes," I moan.

"But who owns this pussy?"

"You do." I moan louder.

"That's right. This is my wife."

Thrust.

"My pussy."

Thrust.

"All fucking mine."

Thrust.

I scream loudly as I come hard. Grant doesn't let up and continues to fuck me like he's never fucked me before.

Finally, I hear Fred start to come next to me onto the bed sheets. Grant must have been waiting for him to come first as his seed starts to spill inside me.

Grant thrusts a few more times before pulling out.

I lie on Fred's bed, a sweaty mess from this unexpected claiming.

Grant stalks over to a pantsless Fred, who suddenly looks scared for dear life again.

"If you fucking go stirring up shit, I'll kill you. Do you understand me?"

"Yes," Fred answers.

"Cara was here for the party idea. Nothing more, nothing less. I don't know what the fuck you have going on here, but I'm the card guy. That's all."

"Got it."

"Good," Grant huffs out.

"Cara, my love, get dressed. I need to take you home and fuck you again."

"Yes, sir."

I scramble to get my clothes on, knowing that somehow Fred believes Grant and, more importantly, I'm about to come all over again back home.

NINETEEN

Grant

"I DON'T KNOW what came over me," I whisper into Cara's hair.

"I liked it." Cara giggles.

"No one gets to see you naked again. No one but me."

"I think you liked claiming me in front of Fred."

"You make me feel crazed. Unhinged. A different version of myself that's been dormant came out."

"I like that I do that to you."

She traces shapes absently into my chest with her fingertips.

We're snuggled together at home on our shared bed. After we got back from Fred's house, we fucked in the living room and then the kitchen before ending up in here, where I made her come two more times.

I felt like a madman watching Fred try to take advantage of my wife. I knew she could handle herself against a man like Fred, but my normally easygoing side went out the window when I saw his proximity to her.

If Cara hadn't intervened in the hallway, I would have killed him and covered it up. Then again, when she reminded me that I couldn't kill him while I made him watch me fuck her, I realized that we had to be Ace and Cara Weston, not Grant and Cara Sinclair.

What a fucking mess all of that was.

I really believe that Fred thinks I was just trying to get ahead and throw a party in his name as an excuse to impress Taby.

"Are we okay?" I ask.

"Yes. Well, you tell me?"

"Yes. I just don't want that to become a habit."

She nods her head against my chest in agreement.

"I love you, Cara. I would say fuck this whole mission if it were up to me. Run away and keep you safe."

Cara sits up and rests her head in one of her hands and keeps the other on my chest.

"Grant. This is the job. We were able to get carried away because of the job. I don't want to be with anyone but you. Did I find that incredibly hot? Yes, I did. And I know you did too."

I let out a long sigh.

"I did."

"Let it be one of many moments that will make up the story of us."

I grab onto her hand resting on my chest.

"I like that."

"Me too. Now we have to take care of our Fred problem."

"I'll make a call to Taby."

"That's good."

I lean forward and place a kiss on Cara's lips. It makes her smile, my favorite thing to do.

"I'll be back," I say.

She rolls over onto her side of the bed, and I get up to call Taby. Slipping on my boxers first, I go in search of my cell phone.

I find it on the nearby dresser and dial Taby's assistant.

"Ace Weston calling. It's important."

"One moment," she says from the other line.

I get put on hold before she says she's transferring me.

"Ace? This better be important," Taby says.

"It is."

"What happened?"

"Fred. Fred Jones. He has home access to all your security systems."

"And you have proof?"

"Pictures in case he makes it disappear."

"Why would he do that?" she cautiously asks.

"It was a misunderstanding. Cara was in his house trying to figure out his interests. It was a poor idea for me to throw a party for him to get more time with you, Cordelia, and the rest of the crew."

"Hmmm."

"It resulted in me finding his security room and then him seeing us there."

"Is this the truth?"

"It is."

"Send the pictures."

I pull the phone away from my head and send her the dozen or so photos that Cara had taken of the evidence. It takes a few minutes for them all to go through.

"Well, this is certainly a problem," Taby says.

"Please let me know if I can be of assistance."

"No need. Thank you for what you've done."

She hangs up, and I wonder what that means.

"What did she say?" Cara asks.

"She asked for details and just said she would be handling it."

Cara shifts on the bed as she sits up against the headboard.

"I think we need to get dressed and wait for activity at his house."

"That's a good idea."

Cara and I both quickly get back into work mode as we move around the bedrooms.

Almost in sync, we each get dressed in our respective rooms and then start putting on our weapons. It takes less than five minutes.

"We should stay in the house. Downstairs, front window will be the best view," she says.

"You don't think we should get closer?"

Cara shakes her head as she leads us downstairs.

"No, I think Taby will be paying Fred a visit and then you."

I hate that she's right. Fred is going to lie through his teeth about our findings. He'll probably even share the truth about how he found us. It'll be up to Taby to decide who she believes.

It's possible she'll head this way to torture the truth out of me or, better yet, kill me on the spot. All scenarios are possible when it comes to this dangerous world.

CARA and I stay seated at the front of the house for hours. One of us will occasionally pace around the house or get a round of coffees, anything to help the time pass.

It feels as if we're watching paint dry on a wall.

This is all part of a stakeout, but at least we're in the comfort of our own fake home to do it. I've run into Cara in the past while we've both been stuffed inside dingy tunnels in the dirt, waiting for deals to be made.

"Remember that time in Michigan?"

Cara perks up.

"When we both discovered we were watching that serial killer who was only killing his patients?"

"Yeah, that time."

Cara laughs as she runs a hand through her hair.

"I hate to admit it, but I am glad you were there. That guy gave me the ick."

I chuckle at the memory.

"He was certainly one for the memory book."

"What about the time we ran into each other at the governor's gala three years ago?"

"Yes, the first time I saw you seduce another man."

Cara gives me a pointed stare.

"Pot, meet kettle," she counters.

I raise my hands in the air in pretend defense.

"Fair enough."

We both walk back to the empty bench in front of the window we've been focused on.

"Hey, Grant?"

"Yeah, love?"

"We should probably talk about what happens after all this."

I nod in agreement as I grip the edge of the bench. Cara takes notice and smirks.

"Or not, if it stresses you out," she teases.

"What I know is that I've meant every word I've said to you."

"Me too."

"I don't think we've really talked about this directly, but after we catch the Marlin, I'm out," I confess.

Cara looks startled by my revelation.

"Do you mean that?"

"I do."

A silence stretches as she takes it in.

"Would you want to leave California?"

"Not necessarily."

Cara glances up at me, and I see the resolve in her gaze.

"But you were planning on it."

"I was, partially."

"Where to?"

I take her hand in mine.

"It doesn't matter. A place isn't a home if it doesn't have you in it. I'll stay in California forever if it means I get you."

I kiss the back of her hand.

"Charleston," she says knowingly.

"It doesn't matter."

"After this is done. Let's talk about it."

"Your family. Work. Your life, Cara, is in California. I know that."

"Not necessarily. I mean..." she starts.

Suddenly, two all-black SUVs pull into Fred's driveway. Men get out of the cars and go around the back to enter. We can't see any further movement from them.

Inside the house, lights start to turn on from the upstairs down to the first floor. Fred must have been upstairs this entire time and is turning them on as he goes to answer the back door or check on the commotion happening.

We may have temporarily turned off his cameras, but there's no way he didn't get them back on as soon as we left.

"What do you think is happening in there?" Cara whispers.

"I think Fred is being killed."

"I think you're right," she murmurs.

Cara crosses her arms over her chest as we both watch on. Light after light gets turned off until Fred's house is pitch black again as dusk rolls through.

"I'm getting restless," she says.

"Something will happen soon enough."

"I know." She pouts.

"Come here," I say.

She walks over to where I'm seated near the window. All our lights are off, so no one can see in.

"Strip."

"What?" she asks through laughter.

"I need another fix of my wife."

Cara's nipples turn to pointy peaks through her bra. I know she likes the idea of me fucking her like this even more than I do. It's good to know that my wife likes to be watched. I may not want to fuck her in front of other people frequently, but I can give her moments of what she wants.

Cara takes off her shirt, followed by her bra. She quickly pulls off her shoes and then her pants and panties next. She stands still as she waits for my directive.

"Play with your pussy."

She starts to play with her breasts first, teasing her nipples and then allows one of her hands to slowly travel down the length of her smooth stomach until it reaches her clit.

"Does the idea of someone watching you outside turn you on?"

"Yes," Cara moans.

She doesn't break eye contact this time. My girl is putting on a show.

"Spread your pussy lips. Show me what I'm missing."

She does as I say, using two fingers. Cara continues to stroke her clit, and her breath turns ragged.

"Come here," I demand.

Pulling down my pants and then my boxers, I remain seated on the bench.

"Fuck me."

She straddles over me so her ass is in view of anyone on the street. It's difficult to see in, but not impossible.

Cara slowly slides onto my cock, and the intrusion stings as she does.

"Are you okay?" I ask.

"Yes, it just takes getting used to every time."

I grip her hips and pull her down fully.

"My little wife can take this giant cock, can't she?"

"Yes," she groans as she holds onto my shoulders.

"Fuck me. I need you to show me how much you want me."

"Only you," she says as she starts her small thrusts on my cock.

"I hope all our neighbors can see you riding my cock. Knowing that you're drenched for your husband."

"Yes, Grant. I love that I'm your wife."

Cara starts to bounce up and down on my cock, and I let her keep control. The way she grinds against me shows how much she's using me for her pleasure. I would happily give this to her every time she needs it.

"Come on, wife. Come on my cock. We've got work to do."

Cara bounces harder, and I suck on her tits, which I

know she loves. She moans wildly, and I can tell she's about to come.

"Yes, I love that," she says.

I gently bite at her nipples before swallowing her breasts in my mouth one at a time. Unable to help myself, I grab her ass and roughly pull her to go faster.

She pants loudly and then screams as her cum finally drenches my cock. I follow behind moments later.

"Good little wife."

She pants as she comes down from her high.

"What do you do to me?" she whispers.

"Hopefully everything."

She laughs lightly before pulling away and getting redressed. I wipe up and pull up my pants and boxers.

Cara snuggles into my side on the bench once she's fully dressed. Only a few minutes pass as we watch the house when one of the SUV doors swings open. A guard gets out, followed by Taby.

She looks around the driveway and glances toward our house. The guard takes notice of it, too, and I watch as they talk to one another while looking in our direction. Thankfully, we know how to stay hidden while still watching through this window.

"What do you think she said?" Cara asks.

"I think we're going to be getting that visit."

"I'm going to start preparations."

"For what?"

"The worst case."

Cara stalks off, and I watch as she begins checking the locations of our hidden weapons throughout the house.

I keep a lookout for any sign of what's to come next.

"Cara," I shout.

"What is it?"

"Fred."

Cara scurries toward the front of the house again.

"What do you mean?" she asks.

"His body."

Cara spots two guards carrying a black bag that no doubt has Fred's body inside. It goes by in a flash as they quickly throw the bag in the back of the SUV. Other guards are standing around, keeping watch.

It's no wonder so many people who work for the organization live in this neighborhood. Truthfully, it all makes sense watching this.

How many neighborhoods can you casually walk out with a giant black bag and someone not take notice? There are so many players living here, and the others know not to cross Taby or Cordelia.

"We're next."

"She isn't going to kill us," I say.

"No, I mean. Someone has to come here next."

"I know."

Cara and I watch as the SUVs peel out of Fred's driveway and ride off into the distance.

"Do you think someone will come later tonight?" she asks.

"I'm not sure."

"I'll heat up something for dinner," Cara offers.

I feel tense, knowing that this isn't the end for Cara and me regarding what happened with Fred. I thought one of the guards would be sent over, but none of them stayed.

Cara starts pulling food out of the fridge as I watch on from inside the living room.

"I'll be in soon to help," I say.

"I've got it," she shouts back.

This is all too simple. There's no way that Taby actually trusts Cara and me this much to have no feedback after her visit to Fred's house.

A loud bang sounds at the door.

I'm so close to it that, somehow, it startles me.

"I'll get it," I shout.

Cara quickly appears in between the kitchen and living room doorway.

"I'll be armed in the kitchen," she says more seriously.

I give her a curt nod.

Looking through the door peephole first, I see it's Brad. I can't let loose, not knowing what he's doing here.

"Hey," I say as I open it.

An exhausted-looking Brad stares at me blankly.

"You okay?" I ask.

"Yeah, I'm okay. Can I come in?"

His hands are inside his front jeans pockets, and he's wearing an oversized brown coat.

"Can I take your jacket?"

"No, I won't be long."

We take a few steps forward.

"Want to sit?"

"Sure."

Brad and I take opposing seats in the living room. One of his legs shakes nervously as he keeps his hands in his pockets and looks around.

"Why did you do it?" he finally asks.

"Do what?"

Brad's face snaps over to mine.

"Fred. Why were you really in his house? How did you know about the cameras? Don't fucking lie to me," he says.

"I didn't trust Fred, and it looks like I was right."

Brad takes it in.

"What are you doing here, Brad? Did Taby send you?"

Brad laughs in disbelief.

"You know, I warned you. I warned you that this wasn't the place for you and Cara."

"What are you doing here?" I repeat.

Brad pauses, and a more serious look appears.

"Taby didn't send me. The Marlin did."

I swallow thickly.

"The Marlin."

"Yeah. You've caught the eye of the Marlin. I hope you know what you're doing."

"What does the Marlin want from me?"

"Here," he says while taking out a piece of scrap paper.

I take it and open it. Scribbled on the paper are the details that Cara and I had found in Fred's office for the meetup.

"What's this?"

"Meetup of the minds, my friend. It's happening."

"Everyone working for the Marlin?"

"That's right. It's going to be a mess."

I study Brad.

"Why do you say that?"

"Taby's crew aren't the only ones coming. She's just been the most helpful to the Marlin. That's why everything has been happening here. The leaders in Chicago and New York failed."

"Failed," I repeat.

"That's right, and Taby stepped up. You have no idea how big this is. Be ready."

"What do I need to do to prepare?"

Brad lets out a tired laugh.

"Think of how you and the wife will not die when you come."

"The Marlin wants Cara there too?"

"It's one big happy family," he says sarcastically.

"Okay. We'll be there."

Brad turns around, walks out the door, and heads down my driveway without another word. He waves his hand briefly near his head as a goodbye.

As soon as I shut the door, I feel Cara walking toward me. I hand over the paper for her to read.

"We did it," she says happily.

"We did."

"Time to notify Dodger." She groans.

"You know he likes it when we call him the director, like we're in a movie," I say with a laugh.

Cara and I head into the kitchen, where her cell phone is lying on the island.

"I don't know what happened to him," she comments.

"What do you mean?"

"We have a history together. I thought you knew that."

I sigh.

"Another time."

Cara dials his office, and once again, his assistant puts us on hold.

"Collins? What do you have for me?"

"That's right. Sinclair is here too."

"Talk," Dodger says.

"We have the Marlin. Date, time, and place where the meetup is happening, officially. It matches what we found in Fred Jones's house."

"Excellent. Do you need a team?"

"Yes, I think that would be best," she says.

"Sinclair, do you agree?" Dodger asks.

Cara looks over at me, waiting.

"Agree. From the sounds of it, there's going to be a lot of players we want. I know the Marlin is the main target, but we can get a lot of the mafia kingpins as well. It'll be huge."

"Send over the details, and we'll be there."

TWENTY

Cara

"I'LL ASK her when this is over," Grant says in the other room.

Carrying my coffee in hand, I tiptoe over to his mainly unused bedroom to see what he's doing.

The door is slightly ajar, and he's sitting on the edge of the bed with his back to me.

"Fisher, I know."

He grumbles at what Fisher is saying on the other line.

"I will. I just can't ask her to up and move her entire life."

Grant laughs.

"I know you did that for Ellie, but that's not how the real world works."

Another silent pause.

"I will. I told you we're on an assignment, and I can't tell you much about it."

Grant sighs.

"You're beginning to sound like me."

I step forward to try and hear better.

"I promise I'll come see you after I'm done in Charlotte."

Grant hangs up and tosses his phone beside him on the bed. I take it as my chance to back away slowly so he doesn't know I was just eavesdropping.

What is he going to ask me when this is over? We have already started talking about our future. I know that I want to be with Grant after our mission ends. I'm not sure why he would be doubting anything that I've said to him.

All of this makes me feel as though I need to talk to someone other than Grant about how I'm feeling.

I like my work; I value what it is I do and the problems I solve to help make the world a better place.

I can admit the truth—I've been running around going a million miles per hour because I haven't had a partner in life. It feels like I found the one person in the world who completely understands me.

I go into my bedroom and lock the door behind me. Stepping into the bathroom, I turn on the shower to help cover up the sounds from the call I'm about to make.

In the bathroom, I sit on the counter near the sink and call one of my best friends, Grayson.

As it rings, I realize that I have more connections in Charleston than anywhere else in the world at this point. Charleston, Hull, and California are where my people are.

"Look who it is," he says.

I rest back on the bathroom sink.

"Hey, stranger, how are you?"

"How am I? Perfect. Talk to me."

"Right to the point?" I say with a faint laugh.

"I know that tone. Something is up, and I'm about to head out on a boat soon."

"I don't want to hold you up."

"Who are you, and what have you done with my friend Cara?"

"Okay, okay, fine."

I adjust my positioning on the counter.

"I fell in love."

Grayson chokes at my words.

"Very funny," I say.

"Okay, wait a second. You fell in love? How? With who?"

"Grant. Grant Sinclair."

"Him?"

"Yes." I sigh.

"Okay, outside of the fact that Harper is going to ask me a million questions about how this happened, I have to ask you this one first."

"What?"

"If you fell in love, why do you sound so melancholy about it?"

"I'm not. What we're working on is almost over, and then we're going to talk about what happens next. He told me that he was planning on moving to Charleston before this happened between us."

"Wait, Charleston? Are you for real?"

"Yeah, he was going to split his time but doesn't need to for us to be together, and so I can keep my company based out of LA."

Grayson is silent on the other line.

"What? Just say it. You have a boat to get to."

"Cara, you know I love you," he starts.

"And?"

"And you're the smartest person I know. Don't tell Liam that," he jokes.

"Okay, but what's your point?"

"You really aren't thinking about this clearly."

I sit upright. Does he think this is a problem?

"How so?"

"You're the boss of your company, which is centered around you. Your parents already split their time between Florida and California. Why couldn't you split your time between LA and Charleston? Hell, I bet you're barely anywhere for that long anyway."

I breathe out a long sigh of relief.

"Thank you."

He chuckles, and I can hear his fiancée, Harper, entering the room.

"Tell Harper I said hi. Can't wait for the wedding!"

"You better be here for it."

"It's a hop, skip, and a jump away from Charlotte. I'll be there."

"Charlotte?" I hear Harper ask.

"Oh, that's right. Hey, Cara, Liam's temporarily working out of a hospital in Charlotte or something. He's been really vague about it."

"Why isn't he practicing in Boston?"

"Looking to make some changes. I'm not sure where he's going to end up."

"Tell Harper her brother better answer my calls so I can get to the bottom of it for us all."

"I promise!" she shouts so I can hear her.

"Alright, I better get going," I say.

"See you soon."

Grayson's right. My life is mine alone, and I can do as I damn well please. I'm not set in California for life. Why can't I keep my business running and finally move to be near friends who feel like family and make my husband happy? He would do anything for me, like not moving.

IT'S a little after seven at night. Grant and I drove to the warehouses early, trying to set up any escape plans that we would need should the meeting go poorly. We scoped it out and found no one else's security or teams were here early.

The mafia must do these types of meetups differently than some of the other criminal organizations that Grant and I are used to dealing with out in the field.

As we wait in the car, I see apprehension in Grant's expression.

"We've got this," I say to be reassuring.

"I know we do," he answers.

Grant grips the steering wheel and taps a few fingers on it.

"I love you," I say.

It gets his attention as he looks over at me.

"And I love you. Always."

He starts to scan the outside of the warehouses again.

"Do you think something's wrong?"

I look around the darkness to see only empty parking lots and warehouses.

"No, I don't think so?"

He hums in consideration.

"Is Dodger here?"

"On the way," I answer.

We keep our eyes out for anyone to arrive. Minutes fly by, and it's almost eight p.m., the time the meetup is scheduled.

"Anything else from Brad or Taby?"

"No, just confirming this is the time and that we better be here."

"Should you text Brad?"

"I will," he answers.

Grant pulls out his phone and texts Brad quickly. As he pockets it, a car arrives and parks up front near the very warehouse where we're meant to meet.

"Let's go," Grant says.

We both hop out of the car and walk toward the empty warehouse. The sound of my heeled boots clacks against the road.

"Do you think it's a trap?" I whisper.

"It couldn't be for us. There are no signs of who we are."

We keep a steady pace as we walk up to the door. Grant pulls the door open, and there's no one inside.

We scan the huge empty building for any sign of life but find no one, not even the person who came in moments ago.

"What the hell?" I ask.

"I'll check over here," he says while heading in the opposite direction.

"I'll check the other side."

This is odd, to say the least. We've been given information about a meetup, and no one's here except us. It feels like a trap.

Shifting in the distance catches my attention. I start to peel back layers of old material hanging from broken flooring above me.

"Hello?" I call out.

A loud crash sounds behind me right as darkness takes over.

"WAKE UP, PRETTY GIRL," a woman's voice says.

My eyes feel heavy, and a weight is keeping me seated. As I try to peel my eyes open, nothing is coming into focus. I must have been hit on the head with something.

"Time to get up," she continues.

"What? Where am I?" I groggily ask.

"At the warehouse still," she answers.

My eyes finally adjust, and I find myself staring at Taby, Brad, and Cordelia. They're all peering down at me as I'm tied up on a concrete floor.

"Why am I like this? I haven't done anything."

"Oh, but dear, haven't you?" Cordelia asks as she steps forward.

Cordelia holds a gun in her hand as she starts to pace along the open space between us.

"I liked you and Ace. Thought you had real potential," she continues.

I struggle against my binds as she talks.

Ace.

My husband.

Frantically, I search around me but see no sign of Grant.

Fuck. This isn't good.

"Where is he? What have you done with Ace?"

"Oh my, what have we done with dear old Ace?" Cordelia asks.

Brad and Taby laugh at my pain.

For a brief moment, I see a look of sadness on Brad's face that makes me want to scream into the abyss.

"We'll get to that."

She continues to pace.

"The whole Fred situation certainly helped your case. I

thought, wow, here are two people dying to come into my fold," Cordelia says.

"Your fold?" I ask, confused.

Cordelia pauses in front of me and tilts her head to the side as she purses her lips together.

"You really don't know, do you?"

"Apparently not. I'm just a housewife."

Cordelia smirks.

"Yeah, and I'm just a diamond smuggler."

My binds aren't held together well, and I'm able to get them to loosen. I'm so close to getting them undone.

I need to get out of here and find Grant. I know there's no way that she killed him. Not yet. He's too useful for her to just murder him. I have to believe that.

"Brad," Cordelia shouts.

He comes running up beside her and waits for his direction.

"Take Ms. Weston to the holding cell."

"With Ace?"

"Yes."

Brad looks back at Taby and then at me.

"What are you waiting for?" Cordelia asks.

"Is that a good idea?"

Cordelia looks angry as her face slowly turns to his.

"Are you questioning my authority?" she draws out.

"No, no, of course not, but if they are really government spies, I was just thinking maybe they shouldn't be together."

"I don't pay you to think."

"Oh, yes, of course," he mumbles as he reaches for me. Brad picks me up underneath my arms and drags me along the concrete away from Taby and Cordelia.

"I tried," he whispers.

"What?" I mumble.

"Get apart. It's the only way you'll be able to take her out."

"Who is *she*? Cordelia?"

"Yes. She's the Marlin."

I gasp.

"The Marlin?"

"I don't have time to explain here."

Brad continues to drag me, and finally, we're in another nearby room off the main open floor. I stand to my feet but keep my hands bound together in case it's a trick. I have no idea whose side Brad's on.

He looks at the door we just came through and then back at me.

"I need a favor," he says.

"What is it?"

"Get Noelle out."

"I..."

"Don't fuck with me. Get her out of this."

I nod in agreement.

Brad starts to take off, but I grab hold of his shoulder.

"Wait. Where are you going now?"

"Did Ace tell you what they call me?"

"Yes. Brad the Bull."

"It's for a reason."

My eyebrows dip inward in confusion.

"Ace is in the back of this room. Get him. Separate. You'll find what you need on the second floor to prove that Cordelia is the Marlin. Tell Ace to get to the roof and wait. My guy will only get there if someone is waiting."

"Your guy?"

"He's going to help."

"Okay," I answer, more confused than ever.

Brad takes off back to where Cordelia and Taby were,

and realization hits—Brad the Bull is going to try and take out Cordelia and Taby. It's a suicide mission that he can't tackle alone.

"Fuck," I mutter.

A groan sounds from nearby. Following Brad's instructions, I go deep into the back of the cell and look for Grant. That's when I still.

There's a trail of blood drops and smears. It's a path that makes me want to vomit. I follow it, knowing that Grant has to be on the other end.

It's dark, far too dark to be in here without any lights on and only the moonlight to guide me. But I know that these marks have to be blood.

"Ace?" I whisper-shout.

Nothing.

"Ace, it's me. Cara."

A groan.

I quickly hurry toward the sound, and that's when I spot him—my love.

I take off the bindings around my wrists and discard them on the ground, then kneel down and get eye level with Grant. He's wounded but not badly. It looks like Cordelia drugged him, and that's why he's so out of it.

I hold onto the side of his face.

"Grant. It's me. Cara."

Grant's eyes flicker in confusion.

"Who are you?" he asks.

"It's me. Cara."

"Cara," he says with a lazy smile.

"Yes, honey. It's me."

He hums, still in a daze.

"How lucky am I that I got even a short amount of time with this woman?"

My heart soars at the sentiment before reality crashes back.

"Grant. I promise... I promise I feel the same way, but we have to get out of here. Now."

"What I would give for just one more taste of her delicious pussy again before I die," he continues.

I hang my head back at his ramblings.

"Up you go," I say as I place my arms under his shoulders and lift him to a standing position.

"Grant. Please snap out of it," I beg.

His eyes shut for a moment as he steadies himself.

"Cara?" he groggily asks.

"*Yes*."

He comes to and suddenly looks panic-stricken as he pulls me into him for a hug.

"Fuck. I'm so glad you're okay," he whispers.

"I'm fine. But we have to leave."

Grant holds onto my shoulders as he separates us.

"How did you find me?"

"Brad. It's a long story. Cordelia is the Marlin."

"I know. She did this to me."

"She knows we're undercover. Brad told me to get to the second floor while you flag down his contact on the roof."

"I'm not separating."

"We have to," I plead.

"I almost lost you once. I'm not doing it again."

I break out of his hold.

"Grant. I'm Cara Collins. I do this for a living. I will not let someone who goes by *the Marlin* be my downfall. I've got this. Now *go*."

Grant hesitates before nodding. We both take off through the room and find a stairwell. The warehouse has four floors.

"I'll see you at the top," I say.

"Wait."

Grant pulls at my arm and swings me into his side. He plants a powerful, all-consuming kiss on my lips. As he breaks away, I can't help but smile.

"Do not die on me tonight," he says.

"I promise. I won't."

I open the door to the second floor and start to run. Looking in room after room, there's no one to be found or any sign of life. Hopefully, Brad isn't steering us in the wrong direction as a distraction. As much of a criminal as he is, I don't think he would do this to us.

I open the second-to-last door to find a briefcase sitting on a table. It's black leather and looks like it's been used for several deals, with how weathered it appears.

Opening it, I find the proof we need. A single file with Cordelia's information and a USB that has a sticky note on it.

Take down the Marlin.

- Brad

I COLLECT the whole briefcase as evidence, then close and lock it shut before running out of the room and down the hall.

Sprinting up the stairs, I finally reach the roof. After searching everywhere, I finally spot Grant.

I let out a loud shriek at who he's with—Dodger.

"When did you get here?" I ask.

TWENTY-ONE

Grant

I'M TRYING NOT to make any sudden moves, but I can't wait to shoot Dodger. As soon as I got to the roof, I saw a pool of blood and a man face down on the ground. Dodger stepped around an air conditioning unit with the gun held high and pointed right at me.

Fucking bastard.

"Dodger. What are you doing here?" Cara asks again.

I see hesitation flicker on her face as she looks at me and back to him.

"I thought you would have sent someone else," she continues.

"I did. They're arresting the Marlin as we speak."

"Okay... that's good. Let's go downstairs to help," she says.

"They don't need our help. Why don't you meet us in the car," he offers.

She can't see the gun he still has pointed at me underneath his coat.

"Okay, Grant can come with me."

"No, I'm afraid I need him in the building with me."

Cara starts to walk toward us.

"Cara. This is a direct order."

"You never call me Cara anymore," she says.

Dodger sighs and pinches the bridge of his nose.

"Get the fuck out of here," he shouts.

"No."

"Collins. I didn't want it to come to this."

The door to the rooftop swings open, and Cordelia and Taby walk out.

"Well, well, well, we're all together at last."

"What's going on here?" Cara asks.

"The director here is on our side," Cordelia answers.

Cara snaps her focus back to Dodger. It's overwhelming to witness the pain in her eyes. They were friends. How could I forget that?

"Dodger. Please don't tell me that's true," she pleads.

"I tried, Cara. I really tried to get you out of here, but you just don't listen. You never do."

Cara's eyes shut, and I can sense tears are threatening.

"Let her go. You have me," I interject.

Dodger's gaze spews venom at me.

"Oh, that's right, Cara and Grant. You two actually got married, and now, what? That's right, decided to actually fall in love," Dodger spits out.

"Dodger, what's happening? Why are you doing this?" Cara begs.

Dodger looks over at Cara and back to me and starts to pace.

"I never was the one meant to get the girl. No matter

how much I tried. After Cara told me she would never consider me as anything else, I can admit, something changed. I became even more focused on work at the agency. Then over the years..." he trails off and pauses.

"Dodger," Cara croaks.

I can see he's breaking my wife's heart from this omission, no matter how much we both want to stop him.

"I asked myself, why am I doing all of this? I became the head of the agency, and for what? A life without women, money, and intrigue. That's when I met Taby and everything fell into place."

"You can still change," I offer.

Dodger laughs loudly as he starts to pace once more.

"I did change. For the better. I may not have your wife, but I did accomplish what I wanted. Now this is it."

Dodger faces me completely.

"You are going to die, Grant Sinclair, as the villain."

"How so? You're the one up here as a traitor."

"No one will know that. Not when you and Mrs. Weston are dead."

"Stop playing with your food," Cordelia says boredly.

"I can't do that," he sneers.

"Kill them, and let's go," Cordelia demands.

Dodger pulls the gun out of his pocket and aims it at me as Taby does the same to Cara.

Out of the corner of my eye, I spot the only sign of hope that we have—Brad.

"Any last words?" Cordelia asks.

"Yeah. Get down," I shout.

Shots are fired from two directions as Cara and I both face-plant onto the concrete roof. It all happens so quickly—one minute, I'm on the ground, and the next, my instincts kick in, and I'm bolting upright and running after Cordelia.

"I'm glad to see you too. Hopefully, next time, it'll be under different circumstances."

"Harper and Grayson's wedding."

"You going to that?"

"Of course! I'm one of the groomsmen," Cara exclaims.

Liam laughs.

"Why would I assume any differently?"

Liam gets to work examining Cara's wounds and getting them cleaned and covered. I'm grateful she'll follow his instructions. When the on-site medic tried to examine her, she refused to be seen despite my pleas.

"All set."

"Thank you." She sighs.

Liam starts to pack up his kit.

"I hear you've been here for a bit," she says.

He looks at her knowingly.

"You know, Grant and I might be moving to Charleston. Part-time at least. Why don't you give it a try?"

"You've been trying to get me to leave Boston for a while."

"I think it'll be good for you. And with you being here... I think you agree."

"I'll think about it."

"Good."

"Can you stay?"

"No..."

Liam gets up, and Cara does the same. He starts to head for the hotel door to leave, and I stay put, leaning against the television stand.

"I think I'll head to Boston and pack up my belongings. Maybe Charleston will be good for me."

Cara squeals and jumps up and down excitedly.

"Can I be the one to tell Harper?"

Liam laughs.

"Don't. I think I want it to be a surprise."

BACK IN CALIFORNIA, Cara and I are watching the sunset on the beach ahead of meeting her parents for dinner.

"It's beautiful out here," she says.

"Only because you're here."

She snuggles in close to me as I wrap the blanket tighter around us.

"It's almost time. We better go talk to them."

"It'll be fine."

"I think it's a good idea you picked a restaurant to do this in," she says.

"Your dad is one of my dear friends. He's not going to hit me in a restaurant because I married his daughter."

"Maybe because you fell in love with her," she teases.

"Perhaps."

I pull her tighter into me.

"Cara? Grant? What's going on here?" Luke shouts.

"Here we go," Cara mutters.

Luke stomps through the sand and gets to us quicker than his wife, Catherine.

"Hi, Dad," Cara says. She doesn't leave my side, and I don't let go either.

"Is this what dinner is about? The two of you together?" he asks.

Luke's hands are on his hips as he waits for our response. We look at one another before turning back to him. Catherine arrives and has a wide smile, seeing us together.

"Yes, it is," I answer.

I finally let go and stand up. Cara follows and loops her arm through mine.

"I'm in love with your daughter."

Luke grins and shakes his head.

"I knew something was up with you two," he says as he pulls me in for a hug.

"You're not mad?" Cara asks.

Luke lets go of me and hugs her as Catherine watches on, giddy.

"Not at all. I always thought the two of you could work, but you were both always such the bachelors."

We laugh in surprise.

"Grant, maybe you can help me with my companies so I can retire."

"Don't get ahead of yourself," I joke.

Luke chuckles.

Catherine pulls me into a hug before taking Cara's arm out of mine and onto hers. She starts leading Cara up the beach toward the restaurant.

"I can't wait until you're engaged so we can start planning a wedding!" Catherine says.

Cara looks back at me, panicked.

"Well, actually..."

Luke realizes what Cara means and sighs.

"Come on, let's celebrate," he whispers to me.

I sigh as we follow behind Cara and Catherine.

"But I'm not going to be the one to tell Catherine you got married."

"We'll leave that to Cara."

Cara suddenly stops, and we all look in her direction.

"Is everything okay?" I ask.

"Let's take a quick photo. We are at our favorite spot. Now it'll be all of ours," she says.

The four of us get together, and Cara pulls out her phone.

"Say, Mrs. Sinclair!" Cara shouts.

"Wait, are you married?" Catherine asks, shocked.

"Let's take the picture." Luke groans.

Cara snaps the photograph, and we all separate. Luke and Catherine start to talk about what's happening as I intertwine my hand with Cara's.

"How are you feeling, my love?"

"Like the happiest person on the planet."

EPILOGUE

Cara

One Month Later

"FUCK," I moan as my fingers twist in Grant's hair.

My legs tighten around his head as his tongue laps up my juices and between every inch of my folds. His palm starts to work my clit, and I know I'm going to be coming any minute.

"Come, love," Grant murmurs before getting back to work.

I rock my hips into his face, and moments later, every inch of me feels like it's coming to life.

"I'm coming," I scream as I hold onto his hair.

Grant doesn't let up as he continues to lick gently as I ride through my orgasm.

My legs widen and fall to the sides of the bed. Grant gets up to his knees and smiles.

"Yes. You make me come like no one ever has," I tease.

"That's what I like to hear."

He collapses next to me on the bed and pulls me into his warmth. The sun shines through the window, reminding me that we can't lie in bed all day.

"We have to get ready," I whisper.

Grant nuzzles his head into my neck.

"We have time," he says.

I giggle as I try to get out of his hold.

"I'm a groomsman. I have to get over to Grayson's house."

"We're his neighbor, my love. It's fine."

Neighbors.

If you had told me six months ago that I would have been completing a mission alongside my dad's best friend, my archnemesis, and all-around thorn in my side, I would have laughed.

I would have fallen over with laughter if you then told me not only would I be marrying him but that I would also be falling in love with the man.

What gets me the most is if you had told me all that and then mentioned how I would be living part of the year in Charleston, South Carolina, surrounded by my oldest and dearest friends, I would have never thought you were telling the truth.

This is all beyond my wildest dreams. I never thought I could be this happy.

After the day we told my parents that we were together and married, they both understood there were some parts of the story we couldn't share. A mutual understanding that somehow we ended up together, and it was the best of all the worlds colliding.

That's what Grant is to me, the epicenter of my world.

It may have started when we decided to tell each other

our lies, but it ended when I believed that I could actually have it all.

"I thought you were trying to get up," Grant teases.

"You're right. We live next door. I can lie with you for a few more minutes."

"If that's so..."

Grant gets on top of me and holds his weight up. I feel his thick cock in between my damp thighs.

"What did you have in mind?" I ask.

"I'd like to fuck my wife."

"Say less."

ACKNOWLEDGMENTS

First and foremost, thank you, reader, for taking a chance on one of my books! I hope you loved Cara and Grant's love story as much as I loved writing it.

Then I have to thank my usual suspects, the ones who have continued to support me and make this experience the best that it can be.

To the best set of family, friends, and early readers—thank you for doing everything you can to support my journey.

To my husband, I'll always be grateful that I picked you as my partner.

Allison and Courtney, thank you for all of your support in making these books shine. To my friends, you know who you are, thank you for all of the support and love you give me with this!

To Steph and Vanessa, with Kat's Literary Services, you two are the best, and I'm forever grateful that we continue to work together on my stories. You both are so vital to my process; I value your edits and thoughts endlessly.

To Sandra with Maldo Designs, thank you for another beautiful cover. It's always a pleasure to see what you'll come up with! Another fitting one that hits the mark.

To Jen, with Grey's Promotions, I'll always thank you for being so helpful with my ARCs, but more than that, as my friend who has believed in my writing from the start.

And to all of the content creators on social media, trust me when I tell you that every post makes a huge difference to an author. I value all of the creativity and support you continue to give me.

Until next time!

ABOUT THE AUTHOR

Angel Anders is a romance author who loves the range of characters and complexities of stories that can naturally unfold when a story comes to life.

When she's not writing, Angel enjoys spending her days along the South Carolina coast with her husband, son, and dog. She enjoys strong coffee, white wine, and curling up with a good book by the fireplace.

www.angelandersbooks.com